The Wi

STAND-ALONE NOVEL

A Western Historical Adventure Book

by

Zachary McCrae

Disclaimer & Copyright

Table of Contents

The Witness..1

    Disclaimer & Copyright..........................2

    Table of Contents...............................3

    Letter from Zachary McCrae 5

Chapter One...6

Chapter Two..14

Chapter Three 20

Chapter Four...28

Chapter Five...32

Chapter Six 35

Chapter Seven 40

Chapter Eight..45

Chapter Nine 51

Chapter Ten 55

Chapter Eleven...59

Chapter Twelve...63

Chapter Thirteen 67

Chapter Fourteen 71

Chapter Fifteen..77

Chapter Sixteen..81

Chapter Seventeen 86

Chapter Nineteen...96

Chapter Twenty 101

Chapter Twenty-One......................................105

Chapter Twenty-Two...108

Chapter Twenty-Three 112

Chapter Twenty-Three 117

Chapter Twenty-Four...123

Chapter Twenty-Five...129

Chapter Twenty-Six 136

Chapter Twenty-Seven..145

Chapter Twenty-Eight..154

Chapter Twenty-Nine 159

Chapter Thirty..165

Chapter Thirty-One 172

Chapter Thirty-Two 177

Chapter Thirty-Three 182

Chapter Thirty-Four 190

Chapter Thirty-Five 195

Chapter Thirty-Six..203

Chapter Thirty-Seven..209

Chapter Thirty-Eight 216

Chapter Thirty-Nine...220

Chapter Forty 228

Chapter Forty-One...238

Epilogue 242

Also by Zachary McCrae 244

Letter from Zachary McCrae

I'm a man who loves plain things; a cup of strong coffee in the morning, a good book at noon and his wife's embrace at night. I want to write stories that take you from the hand and show you what it meant to be someone who tried to make ends meet and find their own way in 19-century United States. I've been this someone for a long time in my life, always looking for my next gig after my parents' sudden death, always finding new friends but somehow not being able to stick with 'em. It's easy to find quantity in your life but what about quality?

At the age of 50, and after my baby boy, Jeb, and my sweet daughter, Janette, went away to study East, with my sweet wife, Mrs. Maryanne Mc Crae, we moved back to my home town and my dad's ranch close to the Rockies. After a series of health issues that have brought me even closer to our Lord, I've officially started writing those stories I always loved to read. I'm tending my land and animals now with the help of Maryanne, and I'm grateful for each day I get to walk on this world we call earth. As the saying goes, "Nature gave us all something to fall back on, and sooner or later we all land flat on it," so I want to take care of it just the way it has taken care of my dad and mom, and my cousins.

My adventure stories are my legacy to my children and to all of the readers that will honor me by following my work. God bless you and your families and our land! Thank you.

Stay safe but adventurous,

Zachary McCrae

Chapter One

Etta Heidelberg was petrified.

The weight of the figure on top of her was almost more than she could bear. The stench of the whiskey on his breath and the clumsy groping way his hands moved over her body made her struggle with every last ounce of strength she had. It was useless.

He was too powerful.

"Just relax, darlin'," he said, his hateful voice close to her ear, "and it'll be over soon. The more you fight, the longer I'll be here. It's all up to you, darlin'."

Tears streaming from her eyes, Etta took a deep breath and forced herself to stop fighting, made herself go limp.

She had no idea how long he was with her. It might have been minutes but it seemed like hours. His body odor was overwhelming, but she knew if she threw up it might make him angry, so she simply turned her head to the side and tried, as best she could, to breathe through her mouth.

She didn't know who he was.

Of course, she knew he was a soldier. That much was obvious but she couldn't tell from the darkened room if he was Confederate or Union. It didn't matter. All that mattered was that he was here with her and he was destroying her, taking part of her with him as he mounted her, forcing himself on her, slamming into her again and again.

When he was finally finished, he collapsed on top of her and said, in a voice that was almost thoughtful, "Maybe I'd be better off if I just went ahead and ended things with you right here and now."

She felt the cold knife blade against her throat.

This was it.

She was going to die.

At that moment, she snapped awake and for a moment, she was completely disoriented.

She took in the coarse blanket, the flickering light from the lantern that she'd accidentally left burning and she lay there, willing her heart to slow down, forcing herself to remain calm.

"Just a nightmare," she told herself. "That's all it was. It was just a nightmare and everything's fine now."

Of course, it was more than just a nightmare, she knew.

It was a memory.

It was a memory of that night, years ago, when a young Etta had woken up in her bed to find a stranger there, dimly outlined by the light from the moon outside her window – a stranger reeking of alcohol and an unwashed body.

The weight of him as he claimed her in her own bed felt like a boulder dropped on her. At first, she'd tried to get him off of her, tried to open her mouth to scream, but he'd whispered, "You call for help, darlin', and you're gonna wind up getting some people hurt, and I'm sure you don't want that. You just need to be quiet and let me do all the work. Once I'm done, I'm out of here and you ain't never going to see me again – but I promise you that you'll never forget me."

She got out from under the blanket and wiped the sweat off her body with a small towel she'd taken to keeping by her bed. The nightmares always came without warning and they always left her feeling drained and completely exhausted.

***

By the time morning came, Etta had managed to pull herself together.

As she'd gotten dressed, she thought about the nightmare, thought about what she saw when she looked at herself in the mirror. There was still some of the pretty young girl she'd been back then, but now there was a weariness in her eyes she couldn't avoid. She'd been told that her eyes sparkled when she laughed.

She couldn't remember the last time she'd laughed, though.

With her long brown hair and high cheekbones, she'd seen how she could still turn the heads of the men in town – but that didn't matter to her. She had one thing on her mind and that was to raise Peter into being the best possible man he could be.

Standing by the stove, she took a couple of eggs out of the skillet and set them down on a plate, next to a glass of milk.

"Peter!" she called. "Breakfast!"

From the room at the end of the small hallway, she heard the sound of movement. She knew from experience that it would be a few minutes before he managed to struggle out of bed and make it into the kitchen.

Sure enough, about five minutes later, Peter came out of his room.

Her attacker had lied when he'd said that she'd never see him again when he was done with her. Even though she had no idea what he looked like, she saw him every time she looked at Peter – the child she loved with her heart and soul and the one good thing to come out of that horrible night.

"Mornin', Ma," he said, sitting down at the table.

She looked at the sandy-haired, pale child that she had kept alive through a frightening childbirth and first few difficult months and, as always, she felt a warmth spread through her that helped her to fight the coldness that night long ago seemed to have left in her soul.

She noticed the way Peter was looking down at his breakfast and said, "Anything wrong, Peter?"

He shook his head and said, "Everything's f-f-fine, Ma."

She was immediately alert. Whenever Peter's stutter began, she knew he was trying to keep something from her.

She left the stove and went over to him, lifting his chin up gently with her hand, and stared at the bruise around his left eye.

She felt sick to her stomach.

"Peter, have you been fighting again?"

He stared at her, his hazel eyes meeting her gaze, and he said, keeping his voice soft and even, "We were playing and I fell, Ma. That's all."

There was a part of her that suspected he might be lying to her, but she didn't want to think about that. Instead, she held onto the words he gave her and nodded.

"All right, then. You know how I feel about fighting. It's not something that I want to see you involved with. You understand that, don't you?"

He nodded.

"Yes, ma'am. I do."

"Anyone who uses their strength to hurt someone is not someone that I want living under the same roof with me. The world is a hard enough place without people out there wanting to cause pain to others."

She watched him move the eggs around on his plate and then take a long drink of milk.

"How's school going?" she asked.

He shrugged. "All right, I guess. Miss Victoria is a little harsh on us, sometimes, but that's just who she is. She's kind of hard."

"She probably just wants all of you to do the best you can and to just behave. I'm sure having a bunch of rowdy boys in the classroom probably makes her have to use a little discipline now and then to keep you young bucks in line."

Peter nodded. "I guess."

"Well, finish your breakfast and then get ready for school. I'm going into town to get some flour and some fabric."

Peter, staring down at his plate, nodded his head again and said, "Yes, Ma."

As she looked at him, she realized that he was probably having a difficult time at school. After all, she was an unmarried woman who had a son, and even though no one had ever asked her about her past, as if sensing it was something she didn't want to talk about, she felt certain that others suspected the truth about Peter's father. After all, it was not an uncommon occurrence after the war.

It doesn't matter who his father is, she thought. *I'm his mother and I've put nothing but love and kindness into that boy – and I know he's going to grow into a fine man.*

She told herself that several times a day – and every night, she prayed to the Lord that Peter would turn out to be the man she wanted him to be.

***

"Hey, Peter," came the familiar, hateful voice behind him, as he stood outside the schoolhouse that afternoon, "did you tell your mommy that I beat you up?"

When Peter turned around, he saw Butch standing there, along with a couple of the kids who always hung around the bully. The smirk on Butch's face made Peter's blood boil but he remembered all the promises he'd given his mother about not fighting and he slowly shook his head.

"I didn't tell her, Butch. That was between you and me."

Butch's dark eyes regarded him for a moment, and then he said, "Yeah, well, that might have been between you and me, but that still don't change what your mommy is. I heard my father saying that you don't even know who your own daddy is because your mother didn't know how to keep her legs closed."

That did it for Peter.

A wave of rage washed over him and before he knew it, he had drawn his hand back, fingers curling into a fist, and he'd hauled off and punched Butch right in the nose.

The banker's son let out a howl of pain and anger and when he pulled his hand away from his nose, blood started spurting out.

For a moment, everything seemed to stop. It was like they were all frozen in place – Peter standing there, feeling a burst of satisfaction over what he'd done to Butch, the others standing next to their friend, watching as he burst into tears, and –

"Peter Heidelberg!"

At the sound of his name coming from Miss Victoria, Peter whirled around to see the tall, pale schoolmarm marching towards him, fury in her eyes. Knowing that he was in trouble, Peter tried to tell her what Butch had said, but his stutter got in the way.

"B-B-Butch s-s-said th-that m-m-m– "

Miss Victoria grabbed him by the ear and started pulling him towards the schoolhouse, where Peter knew his punishment awaited him.

***

Peter watched his mother look up from the note that Miss Victoria had sent home with him; seeing the disappointment in her eyes was nearly enough to make him want to cry. He tried so hard to live up to his mother's expectations, but it was really hard.

She didn't understand what it was like for him – and there was no way he was ever going to tell her, either. He might not have had a man around the house to learn from, but Peter knew that part of being a man was dealing with his problems on his own – and doing everything he could to protect his mother from all the hatred out there in the world.

"Peter, I just don't understand you," she said, softly, shaking her head. "I know that you're a good boy. You're fifteen years old and well on your way to being a fine man. I see it in you all the time – but then you go and do something like this and I've got to tell you, it breaks my heart. With all the violence and fighting and hatred in the world, the thought that my own son would be a part of that makes me just sick to my stomach."

Peter looked away from his mother's gaze, feeling his face heat up. He hated disappointing her, but he knew that if he tried to tell her why he'd hit Butch, she wouldn't understand.

She'd just tell him that it didn't matter what other people said about her. What mattered was that she knew the truth about who she was and she wasn't about to let the opinions of others change how she saw herself.

"I reckon you'd better just go to your room, Peter, and get down on your knees and ask God to forgive you for what you did. Then, tomorrow, you and I are going to go to the Donaldson farm and you're going to apologize to Butch in front of his parents and me. After that, the two of you are going to shake hands and this whole business will be done."

As Peter trudged to his room, head down, he knew there was no way that he was going to apologize to Butch. It was time that he got himself away from here and made his way in the world.

He knew that if he stayed he'd only continue to disappoint his mother and he couldn't let that happen.

Chapter Two

"Now, then, Wilfred," Johnny Steele said, as the two of them rode to Eldin West's farm, "you let me do all the talking, you hear?"

The short, heavyset deputy glanced at the sheriff and rolled his eyes. It was something that Sheriff Johnny Steele loved to joke with him about, considering that Wilfred Stander was as good a deputy as any sheriff could want, but he was also a man of very few words.

Where Wilfred was short and balding, Johnny towered over most men. He had thick brown hair and dark eyes that seemed to take in every detail they saw. Despite his size and his solid build, there was a kind of gentleness to the man that most lawmen didn't have.

Then again, that gentleness quickly disappeared at the first sign of trouble.

They were heading up to pay a visit to Eldin West, a rancher just outside of town. West had had a few run-ins with Steele, and while he was not actually a "bad" man, there were times when he seemed to just charge right ahead and do things without thinking about them.

This was one of those times.

The trail turned to the left and the two men rode through the gate of the West farm. Johnny took note of the four horses out in the field grazing and looked around, studying the farmhouse and the small barn located just to the right.

The porch door opened and Eldin stepped out. He was a big man, with a body that had once been rock-hard but had softened up a bit with the years. His dark eyes glanced from Johnny to Wilfred and settled back on the sheriff.

"Afternoon, Sheriff," he said, his deep voice rumbling. "What can I do for you?"

Johnny flashed him an easy grin.

"Well, I was kind of hoping that you could help me out with a little problem I've got," he said, turning around and looking out into the field and glancing over at the barn. "I guess you've got four horses out there in the pasture, Eldin. That about right?"

The rancher nodded.

"That's right, Sheriff."

"So, all total, how many horses are on the property, Eldin?"

"I got four horses, Sheriff. I just told you that."

Johnny chuckled.

"Yes, you sure did, Eldin. The thing is, I didn't ask how many horses you have. I asked you how many horses are on the property right now. See, Jeremy Carter paid me a visit and told me that the two of you had a falling out and the next thing he knew, he was missing one of his horses. So, I thought that I might just come on by and see how you were and find out if maybe one of his horses might not have wandered over to your property here."

Eldin licked his lips and shook his head, but he didn't meet Johnny's eyes.

"No, sir," the rancher said, quietly. "Only horses I got around here are the ones you see out there."

The sheriff turned his attention back to the barn, looking at the stall shutters; they were all open – except for one.

15

"You know, I think maybe I'll head on over to the barn and just take a little look around. Who knows? Maybe Jeremy's horse came all the way over here and then snuck into the barn without you picking up on that. I reckon something like that could have happened, right?"

Eldin took a deep breath. "Well, I reckon that there might have been a horse showing up here out of the blue this morning and I suppose that the horse might look like one I thought I seen over at Carter's farm, come to think of it. The thing is, Sheriff, when Carter came over to you a-cryin' about me, did he mention that he owes me money?"

Johnny shook his head.

"No, he didn't. What you got to understand, Eldin, is that the law don't care if he owes you money. That's something that you got to settle in court. You don't just take it upon yourself to go and steal a man's horse. That just ain't right."

"It ain't right the man owes me money, Johnny."

"You're right about that and that's why we got Judge Mooney around. He can figure out what to do. In the meantime, though, I reckon you need to take Jeremy's horse back to him and apologize."

Eldin thought about that for a moment, then shook his head.

"I'll take his horse back, Sheriff, but I'll be danged if I apologize to the man. He owes me money."

"Yes, so you said. Take the horse back and then go and tell Judge Mooney your story and if he finds that you've got yourself a case, you'll get your money back – and you might even get an apology from Jeremy himself."

***

As they rode back to town, Wilfred kept looking over at Johnny, frowning. It looked like he wanted to say something but was keeping it to himself.

After a few miles of the sideways glances, Johnny cleared his throat and said, "Reckon you got something that you want to talk to me about, Wilfred."

"Sheriff Brandelle would have run Eldin in, you know. He'd have called the man a thief and that would be the end of it."

Johnny nodded. "Technically, he would be right. I don't see much point in throwing someone in jail if the only thing they did was make a mistake, though. Eldin's not a bad man. He's just someone who thought he got wronged and wanted to see justice done. Only thing tossing him in jail would have done is gotten him embarrassed and made him distrust the law even more than he probably already does. The way I see it, he'll take the horse back and him and Jeremy will go to Judge Mooney and get everything worked out."

Wilfred seemed to think about that for a few miles, then he turned to Johnny and asked, "Where were you before you showed up here, Johnny?"

The sheriff chuckled. This was something that Wilfred had been trying to find out since Johnny first arrived in town. Of course, everyone in Willow's Bend had been trying to learn more about Sheriff Johnny Steele's past, but that wasn't a subject he discussed with anyone.

Some things just needed to stay private.

One of these days, Johnny hoped he'd find someone that he could share his past with – but, for the moment, he simply had to keep his past in the past.

***

When Johnny and Wilfred arrived at the jail, they found Lars McDill repairing one of the front steps leading into the sheriff's office.

Lars was a tall man with thick blonde hair and a quick smile. He was one of the first people who had welcomed Johnny when he arrived in Willow's Bend and there was an easygoing air about the man that immediately made most people relax around them.

"How did it go, Sheriff?" Lars asked, sanding down the edge of the step to remove any stray splinters that might have developed during the repair. He ran his hand over it several times to make certain the job was done properly.

Lars was one of the local handymen and everyone agreed that his work was beyond reproach. He was also one of the most active church members and Johnny knew him to be a vital part of the community, always available to lend assistance to those in need.

"Well," Johnny said, "I think everything is all taken care of. Eldin is on his way to Jeremy's to give him his horse back."

The handyman looked at Johnny for a long moment and then asked, "Do you think most people are basically good people, Sheriff?"

Johnny thought about that for a moment.

"Well, an Indian friend of mine once told me that when he was a little boy, his grandfather told him that all of us have two wolves inside of us. One is good. One is bad. These two wolves are fighting all the time to try to win over the kind of person we are."

"Which wolf wins?" Lars asked.

"His grandfather told him that the wolf who wins is the one we feed the most. I reckon that means we all have good and we all have bad inside of us, Lars, and we're as good or as bad as we make ourselves to be."

"Well, I guess the wolf in you is mostly good, Sheriff," Lars said.

Johnny sighed but didn't say a word.

Chapter Three

There was a storm coming.

Peter's window was open. He could smell the storm out there, could almost feel it, waiting to explode around them.

He lay in bed staring up at the ceiling. His stomach hurt. He was tense. It would be daylight soon and that meant he'd have to face yet another day at school, have to deal with Butch all over again.

It was only a matter of time before he really got into trouble with Miss Victoria. He hadn't told his mother about what the kids at school had been saying about him and about her because he knew it would hurt her.

If there was one thing that Peter never wanted to do, it was hurt his mother.

He knew how hard it was for a woman to raise a child on her own. He'd seen how she'd done everything she could to provide for him – taking in clothes to mend for some of the single menfolk, working the little piece of land as best she could, doing everything possible to make sure that there wasn't a single thing in the world that Peter lacked.

Trouble was – there was one thing that he wanted more than anything and knew he was never going to get.

He wanted a father.

His mother was a strong woman. There no doubt about that. She was probably stronger than a lot of men out there. She might not have been strong in the way that would drive a fencepost into the ground, but she was strong in a different way, in the way that she never seemed to let anything bother her. Whenever something didn't go the way she wanted, she just shrugged it off and went on about her business.

The trouble was, the one thing she couldn't just ignore was her concern for Peter and raising him on her own.

"I need you to be a good boy, Peter," she'd tell him, "so that you can always do the right thing and grow into being a good man. There aren't enough good men in the world, Peter, but I know that you can be one of them."

Peter knew part of what she was talking about was whoever his father had been. He'd tried several times to get her to tell him where his father was and why he wasn't with them but whenever he did, his mother would simply get tears in her eyes and tell him that she wasn't ready to talk about it.

He hated seeing his mother upset.

In the distance, thunder rumbled.

Peter sat up in bed, having come to a decision. It was the hardest decision that he'd ever had to make but the more he thought about it, the more he knew it was the only decision he could make.

As long as he went to school and lived with his mother, Peter was always going to be the cause of trouble for her. The kids at school were always going to say things about her that weren't true and he was always going to have to stand up for her and Miss Victoria was always going to send him home with a note that told his mother that he just wasn't turning into the good man his mother wanted him to be.

Maybe, if he wasn't around, his mother might finally begin to have a life for herself, maybe find herself a good man to settle down with and get some of the happiness that she deserved.

***

Etta got out of bed and slowly stretched.

It had been another restless night. The nightmares had been there. They were always there, taking her back to that horrible night all those years ago. She couldn't remember the last time she'd had a restful night's sleep.

On top of that, she was worried about Peter.

He was a good boy and she knew that he had the potential to grow up into a good man. Even though Etta had not met many good men in her life, she was certain they were out there.

Peter could grow up to be a good man, she knew.

The problem was that he was always seeming to get into trouble. Even though she knew that most of the time it wasn't his fault, she knew people well enough to know how they would interpret things. They would say that he was a troublemaker and a hothead and they would turn their backs on him.

The thought made tears spring to her eyes.

She knelt beside the bed, closed her eyes, and said, "Dear Lord, thank you for the day that is before us. Watch over us as we go about our business, trying to always keep you in the front of our thoughts and our deeds. Watch over Peter especially, Lord – I know he's trying hard to do the right thing and Satan keeps putting obstacles in his path, but with Your guidance, I know that all will turn out well. In the name of the Father, and the Son, and the Holy Spirit, amen."

She rose and took a deep breath. Whenever she prayed, she always felt better. She knew there were people out there who would have made fun of her for what she believed but that didn't bother her. She was rock solid in her faith and she knew that the Lord would always be there for her.

Emerging from her bedroom, she called out, "Peter, I'm going to start making breakfast."

She waited, expecting to hear him grumble about having to go to school. She was met with silence.

"Peter?"

She knocked on his door. When there was no answer, she knocked again.

Still no answer.

Etta opened his door and looked inside. His bed was made, which meant he was awake. That was surprising. Usually, he enjoyed staying in bed for as long as possible.

He was probably starting his chores and was down at the small barn.

Before starting breakfast, she decided she'd better go down and make sure he was all right. It wasn't like him to be so eager to start his morning chores and although she told herself that it was his way of making up for getting into fights in school, she had a nagging feeling that wasn't the case.

She quickly got dressed and headed down to the barn.

The barn door was open but she didn't hear anything from within. When she went inside, she saw Chestnut's stall was empty.

"Peter?" she called out. "Peter, are you here?"

No answer.

In the distance, thunder rumbled and she had a cold, dark feeling forming in the pit of her stomach.

Peter was gone, and it was all she could do to keep from screaming in frustration.

***

Peter was exhausted.

In the distance, storm clouds gathered. They'd been ahead of him all day, slowly approaching. When the storm hit, it would be one of those gullywashers that would stick around for hours, slamming into the area with tremendous force.

He realized he didn't have any idea where to go.

When he'd first set out, all that had mattered to him was getting away from his home, his mother, the school. He wanted to have a fresh start but as the day wore on, he understood that he'd acted without thinking.

"Peter, you always need to look before you leap," his mother would tell him. "You can't always go running off half-cocked, doing whatever you want to do just because you feel like it or it seems like the right thing to do. There are consequences you need to consider, you know."

This was one time he'd wished he'd taken the time to think about what he was doing and had come up with some kind of a plan.

Peter wondered what his mother was doing right now. He hoped that she wouldn't be too worried about him, but he knew that was wishful thinking. She was probably out of her mind with worry; just thinking about that made him sick to his stomach.

He couldn't believe how selfish he'd been when he'd decided to run away.

After a little while, he came to a halt and dismounted from Chestnut. The old horse that he'd taken from the farm let out a whinny of relief and he patted her side.

"I know, girl," he'd said, softly, "I know that you're not used to this and I'm sorry. I just needed to get away from home."

He needed to relieve himself and he moved a little off the trail into some nearby bushes. As he was about to take care of things, he heard voices a short distance away, coming from the right.

The first thought that came to mind was that this might be an opportunity for him. If there were other travelers, he might be able to join up with them. He was fifteen years old and he wasn't afraid of hard work. This might be the godsent opportunity he needed.

About to move forward and introduce himself, something made him be more cautious. This was no time to leap before looking.

He ducked down and peered through some bushes to see two men in a small clearing.

One of the men was tall and muscular, with a face that looked like it was carved out of stone. The other man was on his knees, staring up at the first man.

The first man had a revolver in his hand and it was pointed at the kneeling man's head.

"Coy," the first man said, "what the devil made you think that you could leave Dane Kansas and get away with it? Didn't you stop for a minute and realize stealing from me was a death sentence?"

"Dane, I'm sorry. I don't know what got into me. I guess I saw all that gold and I kind of lost my head. I don't think I was going to keep it, Dane. You know that. I would've brought it back."

The standing man nodded.

"Coy, all you need to do is tell me where the gold is and that'll be the end of it. We won't have to tell anyone else what you did and we can forget all about this," the armed man said, his voice soft and convincing. "It'll just be between us."

The second man nodded and said, "Okay, then. You give me your word that you won't kill me after I tell you where the gold is and I'll take you there."

The first man nodded.

At that moment, a jackrabbit darted out of the bushes near where Peter was concealed; both of the men turned to look in that direction.

Everything seemed to slow down, then.

Peter saw the second man jump to his feet and charge at the figure with a gun. There was a brief struggle and then, the sound of a gunshot.

The man who had been called Coy fell to the ground.

The paralysis that had been holding Peter broke, then, and he stood up.

As he did so, just for a moment, the first man saw him and their eyes locked.

Peter had never seen eyes like this man had – dark and cold and dangerous. They were eyes that looked like they belonged to a snake or a lizard.

"Come on out, boy," the man said.

For a moment, Peter almost obeyed him – and then, without thinking, he turned around and ran away, back towards Chestnut.

Chapter Four

Johnny sat at his desk, staring out the window at the threatening sky. Thunder rumbled in the distance and he knew they were in for a major downpour. He hoped Eldin had made it to Jeremy's ranch with the stolen horse and that the two men might have come to some kind of understanding.

He doubted it, though. He was familiar with both men and they were each as stubborn as a couple of mules, caught in quicksand but refusing to let themselves be pulled out.

Thunder rumbled again, and his hand moved down to the badge pinned to his chest.

It had been George Stern's badge – his best friend, who had been the previous sheriff, until he'd been killed by Indians. At least, that's the story Johnny had been told, though he wasn't sure he believed it. The locals in this area were all friendly and he couldn't imagine any of them going after George and killing him.

Then again, when it came to Indians, Johnny had been warned, time and time again, that they couldn't be trusted. He didn't have any bad experiences with them but he also knew others who had.

"Just because you ain't never been kicked by a horse, Johnny, don't mean horses don't kick," Wilfred had once told him.

Right now, Wilfred was over at Carl Montgomery's workshop, helping the blacksmith fix some loose planks in the floorboards. Johnny couldn't help but smile, thinking about the deputy and how much of a help he'd been when the townspeople had decided that Johnny had to pick up the badge and take George's place.

This wasn't something that he'd planned on – but then again, very little in his life had gone according to plan.

Another rumble, this one was much closer, sent a tremble through the very floorboards of the jail.

He got up to look out the door when it flung open before he could reach it.

Etta Heidelberg came bursting in, her pale features a mask of panic.

Johnny looked at the attractive woman, taking in her dark hair and eyes – eyes that were filled with worry.

"Sheriff, you have to help me," she said, her words coming together so quickly that he almost couldn't understand her. "It's Peter. He's run away from home. I don't know where he is or what's going through that mind of his. If anything happens to that boy, I'll die."

Johnny took in the sight of her and nodded. He kept his voice calm, level. He needed to reassure her.

"Calm down, Etta. Peter's a smart boy and even though it don't make sense, him running away, we'll find him and bring him home."

Etta took a deep breath and slowly nodded. Tears streamed down her face.

"Thank you, Sheriff," she said. "I don't know what I'd do without you."

Johnny couldn't help but feel a pang of guilt as he looked at Etta. He knew she was a single mother, struggling to make ends meet, and he couldn't help but feel an attraction towards her. Now was not the time to think about that.

He had a job to do, and finding Peter was his top priority.

"You head on home," he said, "and let me handle things. I'll get Wilfred and we'll go out looking for him. Is he on foot or did he take one of the horses?"

"He took Chestnut."

Johnny kept his features impassive but he didn't like the fact the boy was on horseback. That meant he'd be able to cover a greater distance.

Johnny grabbed his hat and gave Etta what he hoped was a reassuring smile as he said, "Don't you worry, Etta. We'll find him and bring him home."

***

Dane Kansas sat on his horse, staring at the clouds that were now rapidly approaching. The wind had picked up and there was a dark, ominous feel in the air.

He had to find the boy who'd seen him kill Coy – and he knew he had to do it fast.

He had no choice but to kill the boy. Dane felt anger at the boy for putting him in this position. Killing a man was one thing, but this – this was different.

Still, if he didn't do what had to be done, the authorities would be told what Dane had done and they'd come after him. The next thing he knew, he'd be dancing at the end of a rope; he wasn't about to let that happen.

He spurred his horse on, determined to find the boy and take care of the problem as quickly as possible. As he rode along the trail the child must have taken, he kept his eyes peeled for any sign of his quarry.

Dane gritted his teeth, hating what the danged nosy boy was forcing him to do and knew when he finally caught him, he'd simply have to make it as quick a job as possible.

In the distance, lightning flashed across the sky.

***

Johnny was about to head out into the storm when he stopped and turned to face Etta.

"Any idea why Peter would take off like that? Did he say anything about where he was going? Did anything happen that might have made him run off?"

Etta sighed. "Miss Victoria sent a note home saying that he's been getting into fights in school. I don't understand that. I've made sure that Peter knows that I don't approve of fighting, of any kind of violence."

"It must be hard on the two of you," Johnny said, his brow furrowed. "A boy needs a man to teach him how to handle himself in the world."

Etta nodded and Johnny saw the tears in her eyes. "I know, but it has to be the right man."

For a moment, he was tempted to ask her about Peter's father but he felt it wasn't the right time or place.

Etta and Johnny stared at each other, and he felt a tension between them that had never been there before. Finally, he cleared his throat and said, "I need to go and find Peter. The storm's almost here and he doesn't need to be out in that."

Etta gave him a timid smile and nodded.

"Thank you, Sheriff. Thank you for everything that you're doing."

He nodded and headed out into the impending storm.

Chapter Five

Peter clutched his horse's reins tightly as he rushed through the stormy night. The rain beat against his face. He could barely see the trail ahead of him. Heart pounding, he tried to rid himself of the image of a man being killed in cold blood, but it seemed like every time he closed his eyes he kept seeing that horrible moment over and over again.

All his plans for running away were gone now. He knew that he had to get back home, had to find the sheriff and tell him what he'd seen. He didn't know whether or not the killer was following him, but Peter knew he had to assume that he was not safe.

Thunder boomed through the night and there was a bright flash of lightning, illuminating the dark sky. Peter looked behind and saw a figure on horseback coming towards him. Although the rain and the darkness made it impossible for him to make out any details, there was no doubt in his mind that it was the killer coming after him.

Chestnut was giving him everything she had but he didn't know if it was going to be enough. When he looked again, it seemed as if the killer was even closer now – with the barrel of his revolver aimed right at him!

***

Dane was furious.

The rain pelted his face, blinding him. All thoughts of guilt at killing the boy were gone now. He'd been pursuing the boy for what seemed like hours.

A flash of lightning showed him the boy ahead of him on the trail and Dane took out his revolver. Urging his horse forward, Dane heard the sound of the animal's hooves pounding along the muddy ground. They were gaining on the boy and Dane was almost close enough to finally put an end to this chase.

At that moment, it seemed as if the sun had exploded in the night. Lightning shot from the sky, slamming into the tree directly ahead of them. Dane found his horse rearing in sheer panic, throwing him out of the saddle.

He slammed into the ground. The air was knocked out of him and by the time he got to his feet, his horse had bolted down the path, heading back the way they'd come. A wave of dizziness washed over him and Dane dropped to his knees, waiting for the sensation to pass.

There was an explosion of thunder and Dane howled in rage. He'd been so close to finally ending the chase and now, he was going to have to deal with the busybody who was, even now, escaping into the night.

All was not lost, though. Dane knew the boy was probably going to head to the nearest town and all Dane had to do was make certain he took care of the boy before the law caught him. Even if he told the sheriff what he'd seen, if Dane could kill the boy before they went before a judge, there would be no witnesses to Coy's murder.

Dane took a deep breath, shook his head, and began the long trek to town.

***

Heart pounding in his chest, Peter saw the killer aiming his gun at him and knew that his life was over. There was nothing that he could do. He was about to die.

The fear and adrenaline that had been his companions since the murder were gone. In their place was resignation. He'd done the best that he could and it hadn't been enough.

After all, he was just a kid and was definitely no match for a seasoned killer.

"I'm sorry, Ma," he whispered. "I love you."

At that moment, lightning shot down from the sky, striking a large oak directly in front of Peter's pursuer. The bolt smashed the tree in half and it crashed to the ground, blocking the killer from further pursuit.

Then the killer was thrown from his mount and moments later, the horse went running down the path, away from Peter.

Relief flooded Peter and he urged Chestnut on.

He didn't know how long it would take his pursuer to find another mount and come after him but it didn't matter. By that time, Peter would have returned home and told Sheriff Steele and anyone else who would listen what had happened.

Surely the killer wouldn't be stupid enough to try to come after him once he was safely back in town, Peter thought.

And yet, there was a sudden feeling of dread washing over him that made him think that things might be far from over.

Chapter Six

As Johnny rode through the storm, his thoughts kept returning to the frantic terror on Etta's face as she worried about her son. Although the sheriff tried to stay focused on looking for any trace of where the boy might have gone, he couldn't keep from thinking about Etta.

From the moment that she and Peter had come to town, Johnny had been aware of her. There was something about her that he found very attractive. It wasn't simply the fact that she was beautiful, though. It was more than that – something on a deeper level.

He'd seen it a couple of times in her eyes. There was a strength to her that couldn't be denied. At the same time, there was a wariness when she was around him – or anyone else, for that matter. It was as if she couldn't quite bring herself to trust anyone.

He kept his eyes open, holding his lantern high as he tried to determine whether or not Peter might have come down this way. If the boy had run away, the odds were that he'd be looking for somewhere he could have a future and that meant the nearest outpost, which was about ten miles to the east.

Johnny wondered what had caused the boy to suddenly up and run away. From what he'd seen of the relationship that mother and son had, they were very close. He couldn't imagine it was anything that Etta might have done that would have caused Peter to take off for parts unknown.

More than likely, it had been some of the comments that had been made about the boy and about his mother. Johnny had overheard some of the locals making remarks, although they'd quickly turned silent when they saw the disapproving look on his face, he knew.

Still, what the parents probably said behind closed doors when their children were around likely got back to the boy.

Johnny knew from experience the difficulties Etta faced when raising a child on her own. His own sister, Grace, had been forced to raise her daughter on her own, after her husband was killed in the war. Johnny had been there for the two of them as much as he could but when scarlet fever took mother and child, he'd decided he needed to get away from the place that held such sorrow-filled memories.

Lightning flashed across the sky, then, and Johnny's attention was directed to some snapped branches just off the main trail. From the way they were hanging, they must have been damaged pretty recently – if it had been longer than that, they would probably have fallen to the ground with the passage of time.

He directed Gunpowder, his horse, to move from the trail into the brush.

***

The storm was finally letting up.

Peter was fairly certain he was close to leaving the side trail and getting back onto the main trail. At first, he'd wanted to ride just along the main trail, but he realized that he had no idea if his attacker had another mount nearby or if he'd managed to catch up to the horse, so he decided his best chance was to simply head on back to town.

The sooner he found himself back in town, the sooner he'd be able to stop looking over his shoulder.

If there was one thing Peter knew, it was that Sheriff Steele would make sure that the outlaw murderer didn't show his face in town. From the moment that he'd shown up as sheriff, Johnny Steele had been the perfect example of everything that a man should be: strong, confident, and always willing to help out those in need.

There had been a couple of times when he'd been in town with his mother that Peter had wondered what it would be like if he ever found out who his father was. No matter how often Peter tried to get his mother to tell him what he wanted to know, she was always silent on the matter, telling him that she'd tell him when he was older.

He had a feeling that she had just been saying that and she had no intention of following through on her promise.

Of course, Peter knew his mother probably had a good reason for not telling him who his father was. He was probably someone who wasn't a decent man, like Billy Jeffrey's father, who was always drunk in the saloon. If that was the case, though, why had his mother even gotten involved with whoever his father was?

He was jolted, then, when Chestnut stepped into a rut and pitched forward, unseating Peter. He landed on his side, smashing into a thick tree root jutting from the ground. As he rose to his feet, there was a loud crash of thunder and before Peter even knew what was going on, Chestnut bolted down the path.

"Chestnut!" he called. "Chestnut, come back! Whoa! Whoa, Chestnut! Whoa!"

Within seconds, the horse had vanished into the night.

Peter stood there for a moment, then sighed and began the trek back toward town.

***

Listening to the sound of the storm, Etta knelt by Peter's bed, head bowed in prayer.

37

She'd known it would be pointless to try to get any sleep – not while her little boy was out there. Every time there was an explosion of thunder, her heart would race and she'd clench her hands into fists.

She knew Peter had a good head on his shoulders and that he wasn't likely to do anything foolish, but there were any number of dangers out there at night – especially during a storm like this.

Why on earth had he gone and done something like this?

She knew the answer, though. It was obvious. The boys at school must have been teasing him about having no father and things had just reached the end of his patience. She'd been wrong not to listen to him, not to let him explain.

The problem was that Etta hated violence. As far as she was concerned, there was never a reason for violence, never an excuse to cause someone else pain. She knew, however, that her views on fighting had been caused by what had been done to her.

Maybe telling Peter some of her past might have kept him from running away – but how could she have told him that he was the product of someone doing the unspeakable to her?

She sighed, shaking her head. There was no point in looking to the past for answers at the moment. Right now, she needed to focus all her attention on Peter, and on praying for his safe return.

"Lord," she said softly, "I place Peter's life in Your hands. When something horrible was done to me, You looked down and gave me something beautiful and wonderful to keep in my life. I ask You now, Lord, to watch over Peter and to bring him back to me, safe and sound, so that he can serve You, Lord."

Etta took a deep breath and rose from where she'd been kneeling, knowing all she could do for the moment was simply wait.

***

The storm had finally passed.

Johnny dismounted from Gunpowder, moving carefully along the side trail. Although the rain had completely removed all traces of anyone who had been along the path, there were still telltale signs that something had passed through this way recently. Of course, there was no guarantee that whatever had passed had been a boy and his horse. It might well have been a deer or even a bear, although there were not many sightings of bears in this part of the forest.

The lantern's light revealed what looked like a passageway through some thick bushes, possibly leading to a clearing. It was possible the boy had gone this way, hoping to find some shelter; the sheriff's pulse quickened, hoping that things would soon be resolved.

Nothing would please him more than being able to reunite Peter with Etta.

As Johnny had suspected he would, he soon emerged into a clearing. At that moment, the moon appeared from behind some clouds, shining down upon the sheriff and the woods.

At that moment, his eyes fell upon a figure lying face down upon the ground and Johnny's legs nearly gave out on him as he realized he'd found Peter – and that the boy was dead.

Chapter Seven

Dane was close to town.

During his ride, he'd been thinking about the boy and what he was going to do. The more he thought about it, the more he realized the boy probably hadn't gotten a good look at him. Even if he had, as long as Dane was careful about how he presented himself in town, there was a good chance no one would be able to figure out that he was a killer who had shot Coy.

As an outlaw, he'd learned the fine art of how to disappear into the background when trouble showed up. One of the biggest mistakes outlaws that he'd known in the past had made was being full of themselves, wanting to go into town and make themselves look like they were special and powerful.

That was a great way to get the eyes of the law focused on them.

Dane was smarter than that. When he showed up in town, he'd simply go into a saloon, take a table in the back corner, drink his whiskey, and just keep his eyes and ears open. A man could learn a whole lot about a town and what was going on simply by keeping his head down and being observant.

It was a hard world out there and hard choices had to be made all the time. Once again, he felt rage at what this fool boy was forcing him to do – cheating the youth from experiencing so many things in life.

It didn't matter.

The boy had to die.

***

Johnny found his hands shaking as he approached the body.

His thoughts whirled as he wondered just how he was going to be able to look Etta in the eye and tell her that her son was dead. It was going to destroy her and it was all he could do to keep from letting out a cry of frustration.

When he reached the body, however, something was wrong.

This couldn't be Peter. Peter was a fifteen-year-old boy, and the fallen figure on the ground in front of him was an adult man. Johnny knelt down and rolled the man over.

He saw the wound in the man's chest – a gunshot wound.

Murder.

On the one hand, Johnny felt a huge wave of relief that Peter wasn't dead. Moments later, though, the sheriff realized Peter might still be in an incredible amount of danger. There was a dead man here and that meant there was a murderer somewhere out there – which meant that no one was safe.

Since becoming sheriff, he'd never had to deal with this kind of violence. Mostly it was a matter of hauling in someone who had had too much to drink or deal with the occasional stolen horse or cow. This was an entirely new area for him and knowing that Peter might somehow be involved added urgency to the situation.

The first thing he had to do, he knew, was find Peter.

***

Peter recognized the path he was on and knew he was close to town.

He stumbled forward, exhausted. After he'd witnessed the killing, he'd been driven forward by fear. Once that passed, though, all he could do was simply put one foot in front of the other, slogging through the mud, tripping over the occasional root and fallen tree limb.

As he passed through some bushes overgrowing the path, their branches pulled back and then snapped forward, striking him in the face. Doing his best to ignore the sudden sharp stinging, he kept thinking about getting to the safety of the town and being with his mother again.

He couldn't believe that he'd been so foolish as to run away and leave her alone. At the time, the only thought on his mind had been to put distance between the humiliation he felt at school and everything else, but now he knew that it had been a cowardly thing to do.

Even though his mother refused to tell him anything about his father, Peter was pretty sure the man would not have been a coward. There had been a war going on, of course, and Peter wondered if his father was a soldier and if he was, if he had been killed in the fighting. If that was the case, he understood why his mother would have kept that from him. She would have thought she was protecting him.

That was part of the reason that he'd run away, too, he realized. His mother kept trying to protect him and whenever he asked questions about his past, she simply refused to talk about it. Sadness seemed to fill her eyes when he tried to find out more about who he was and where he came from – and eventually, he learned to stop trying to find out answers.

He never stopped wondering, though.

Peter tripped over a thick branch on the path and fell forward. As he did so, he put his hands out to brace himself and let out a muffled cry. The moment he did, he realized the sound had come out louder than he'd expected, shattering the silence of the forest after the storm.

At that moment, he heard the sounds of movement suddenly coming toward him and he dove off the path into the thick underbrush.

***

Dane spotted movement ahead of him.

It was obviously the boy, he realized. Rather than rely upon stealth, he shot forward, pushing his way ahead toward where he'd seen moving branches through the underbrush. His gun was drawn and he was ready to use it at a moment's notice. All he needed was one clear shot.

If there was one thing that Dane knew, it was that the countless hours he'd spent practicing with his revolver had made him one of the deadliest outlaws in the territory. Some men were fast when it came to drawing their weapon and others were accurate.

Dane was both.

He could have his revolver in his hand and send a bullet into the heart of any man standing in front of him before the fool even realized that he was dead.

At the last moment, though, the outlaw forced himself to slow down and take a breath. While it was true he was only going after a boy, he also knew charging forward recklessly could result in some serious problems. After all, Dane had only been fourteen when he'd set out with a stolen gun and some supplies to make his way in the world, far from the orphanage where he'd been treated like trash.

There was no reason to think the boy wasn't armed, and that meant he had to move cautiously. He hadn't survived this long in the world of the lawbreakers without understanding that nothing could be taken for granted – not even the simple act of tracking down a young boy.

Taking a deep breath, he moved forward, then – slowly, carefully, making certain each step he took was solid, cautiously avoiding any branches or twigs snapping at his approach.

Now that the storm had passed, the clouds scuttling across the sky were nearly all gone, leaving the full moon overhead to cast light down upon the scene below. Dane moved slowly, knowing that he was now an exposed target.

He was also aware it would make the boy just as visible.

Dane moved around the side of a large oak tree which had thick bushes growing alongside it. He crouched down and quietly moved the branches of the bush aside until he had an opening he could see through.

The boy was bent over, moving forward.

As the outlaw watched and the figure cloaked in shadows rose, he realized he wasn't seeing a boy.

He was seeing a man.

More importantly, however, the light from the moon overhead was reflected off the sheriff's badge the man wore.

Dane silently cursed. As much as he had dreaded having to kill the boy, he knew killing a lawman was much, much worse. That kind of reckless action would have an entire town forming a posse and coming after him, and that was something he intended to avoid.

For the moment, tracking down the boy was going to have to wait.

He was a patient man, though, and he knew that, when the time was right, he'd be able to make sure that any witnesses to his misdeed were taken care of.

Chapter Eight

Peter was exhausted.

He kept looking ahead for some sign of Chestnut but it looked as if the horse was long gone. That made sense. As big as a horse was, they were still considered prey animals and that meant most of them were nervous creatures. The storm had kept the horse nervous and Chestnut probably had picked up on the panic that was inside Peter himself as he tried to keep one step ahead of the murderer.

Even now, every single noise, whether from the rustling of the branches as their water-laden leaves created movement and sound or from some woodland creature being spooked, had him shooting his head around to make sure that he wasn't in the crosshairs of the killer in the storm.

Peter hoped that Chestnut had had sense enough to make it back to the farm. The last thing in the world he and his mother could afford to lose was such a precious animal and if it turned out that Chestnut was gone, that was going to be something else he'd be feeling guilty about.

Right now, of course, he was feeling guilty about having run away from home, having left his mother on her own. What had he been thinking? He was sure she was out of her mind with worry and knowing he was the cause of it made him sick to his stomach.

More than that, though, he knew that he might have put himself and his mother in danger. No matter what happened, Peter was not about to let anything bad happen to his mother. He was going to do whatever it took to make sure she stayed safe.

Suddenly, Peter heard a branch snap nearby and his heart raced. This was not the sound of an overloaded limb collapsing under the weight of the storm – this was what it sounded like when someone stepped on a fallen twig.

There was sudden silence.

Peter took a deep breath, then carefully moved over to a large oak tree. It was an old one, which meant it could provide enough cover for him to use to hide behind. Right now, all that mattered was getting out of sight from whatever – or whoever – had made that noise.

Moving as quickly and as quietly as he could, Peter went over to the tree and slowly eased around the massive trunk, doing his best to blend in with the shadows of the forest.

There was another snapping sound and someone drew closer.

***

Johnny's gaze moved to the side of the trail, where he saw several broken branches on the ground. Lifting his lantern higher, he saw where a few limbs that were high off the ground were broken – as if someone had pushed their way through them.

He moved forward, cautiously.

There was a lost boy out here, after all – and there was a killer, too. The last thing the sheriff needed to do was announce his presence to whoever had killed that man back there. As he dismounted from his horse, he turned down the lantern's light, then set it on the ground. Johnny needed to move ahead cautiously; that meant using the light from the moon as his only illumination. Tracking down a murderer while holding a lantern might as well be setting himself up as target practice.

After a few feet, he found himself in the middle of another small clearing. There were several large oak trees surrounding him, but Johnny kept his attention focused on the ground before him. There was just enough light for him to make out what looked like footprints leading to an oak tree just to the right of him.

He couldn't tell, because of the muddy ground, whether it was a young boy's footprints he was tracking or a grown man's – which was why he drew his revolver and slowly approached the oak.

***

Someone was coming.

Peter's heart pounded. Every instinct in him was telling him to just push forward and run away, but he stayed where he was. There was a chance the killer might actually just pass him by if he didn't attract any attention.

He closed his eyes and began to silently pray.

His mother had taught him that God was always watching over folk – knowing when they did good, knowing when they did bad, and knowing when they were in trouble. Right now, Peter reckoned he was in a lot more trouble than most people and he hoped that God was looking down on him and wanting to make sure nothing happened to him.

It wasn't really himself he was worried about, though.

Peter knew the world was not a very safe place at times and he grew used to that. He knew life wasn't fair, too. If it was fair, he wouldn't be the one getting into trouble in school when the bullies made comments about his mother.

He just couldn't bear the thought of what would become of his mother if anything happened to him.

He knew she'd probably blame herself, even though none of this was her fault. All of this was on him. He was the one who'd gotten into a fight and he was the one who had decided that it was best for him to run away from home.

Now, however, all he wanted was to simply get safely to town and be with his mother and never do something this foolish again.

He saw a figure emerge and head towards him. The full moon was behind the man, making it impossible to see any features, but the one thing Peter saw quite clearly was the gun in the man's hand ...

***

The moment that Johnny spotted Peter, he knew the boy was seconds away from making a run for it.

He could practically read the tension in the young boy's body and before he could think of what to say, how to react, Johnny's gaze fell to the ground near where the boy was standing. Through the mud covering the ground, there was a glint of metal – and it only took a second to realize it was an unsprung bear trap.

More than that, though, it was right next to where Peter stood. If he made a move in the wrong direction, it would clamp shut on him and probably cripple him for life.

"Easy there, boy," he said, doing his best to keep his voice calm and gentle. The last thing he needed was to scare the boy into running. "I just need you to stay right where you are so that I can – "

He didn't get a chance to finish his sentence.

A split second before Peter went to move, Johnny saw the muscles tense, saw the boy look to his right, and then he threw himself to the side to try to make it past Johnny.

Before he'd moved, however, Johnny had already been prepared. He lunged forward, grabbing Peter by the wrist and pulling him with all his might to the left, away from the trap.

Both man and boy fell to the ground then, landing in the mud. Peter tried to push his way free from Johnny, but the sheriff held him tight.

"Let me go!" Peter yelled. "I ain't gonna tell no one what I saw. Just let me go!"

At that moment, a branch right above where Peter had been standing snapped, falling to the ground. It landed on the trap, which slammed shut a moment later.

***

Peter realized that the bear trap could have crippled him for the rest of his life. It might even have killed him.

He also realized that the man who had saved his life was not the man that he'd been running from. As he got to his feet, he saw the badge on the man's vest and he looked up into the face of Sheriff Johnny Steele.

He hadn't taken more than a step when a sharp pain went through his ankle and he collapsed.

"I think I twisted something when I fell," Peter said. "I'm sorry. I didn't even see the trap."

"Mud covered up most of it. Only reason I saw it was moonlight bounced off a little metal there," Johnny said, going over and helping the boy to his feet. "Probably just got yourself a sprain here. We'll get it looked at when we get back to town."

"I reckon you came out here looking for me," Peter said, embarrassed. "My ma sent you, didn't she?"

The sheriff gave him a long, searching look, then finally nodded. "Yeah, she did. You know that she's worried sick about you, don't you? She's practically out of her mind with worry."

Peter sighed, shaking his head. "I never meant to do this," he said. "I just wasn't thinking right, I guess. I reckon I'm in a whole lot of trouble."

Sheriff Johnny frowned and said, after a moment, "I reckon you might want to tell me what it is that you saw, Peter – and who you thought I was when you said you wasn't gonna tell no one."

Chapter Nine

Dane sat in the back of the saloon, keeping to the shadows. The place was busy and before settling in, he'd looked around carefully at the clientele, wanting to make sure that he didn't recognize anyone.

For what he needed to do, he had to make sure no one from his past was around to point out just who he was.

Sipping his whiskey, he listened to the men at the table beside him. Both of them were well on their way to being drunk – with voices that were loud and no care taken to make sure they weren't attracting attention.

They wouldn't have lasted two days with Dane's gang.

"I'm telling you right now, Joseph," the first man, a balding older customer, said, pointing his finger at his companion, "that damned boy is going to be nothing but trouble for Miss Etta. He's got a temper on him and he's always looking for a fight."

The second man scratched his thick black beard and nodded. "Don't I know it!" he said. "From the minute they came to town, you could see that she was a good woman, obviously, but that boy of hers was ready to throw down his fists at the drop of a hat. I'm not surprised that he just run off like he did."

"Trouble is, Sheriff Johnny's out there looking for him now. Town needs its sheriff right here and not chasing after some fool kid who doesn't know any better than to run off in the middle of a danged storm."

Dane kept his attention on his drink, not wanting either man to know just how much he valued the information they had just given him.

So, it looked like the boy might be considered a troublemaker. That was good news. It meant that not everything he said might be taken as gospel. He also learned the boy's mother was named Etta and from the way the two men talked, it didn't seem like there was a man involved with her, other than the sheriff who was out looking for the boy. That was definitely good news.

Of course, that might not be good news for the sheriff and the boy, but at least Dane knew he'd only have to kill two people and not more than that. After that, all he had to do was find out where Coy had hidden his gold.

***

"I think that you'd better tell me just what's going on, Peter," Johnny said to the passenger riding behind him on Gunpowder. "I got me a dead body in the woods and I got you thinking that I was going to kill you. Who did you reckon I was?"

The two of them rode in silence for a little while before Peter said, "I thought you was the guy who killed that man."

Johnny kept from letting out a curse under his breath. He'd hoped that the boy hadn't actually witnessed the crime. No one should have to see a man get murdered – especially someone young and not yet experienced in the world.

"Did you get a look at the fella who did it?" he asked.

"No, sir. I mean, I saw a little bit but it was dark and I really wasn't paying attention. I just stumbled to what was happening, that's all."

"You reckon the killer saw you, Peter?"

There was a pause and then the boy said, in a low, frightened voice, "I think he might have. Yes, sir."

Johnny took a deep breath. This was bad. He knew that any man who went around killing wasn't about to risk letting a witness stay breathing for too long. There was a chance the man might already have left the area, heading to wherever it was he was heading, but it was far more likely he was still around, wanting to find out just what had been seen – and, more importantly, where the witness might be found.

Johnny knew he was going to have to keep the boy and his mother safe – and at the same time, he was going to have to track down a killer.

***

Dane, lying in bed in the rooming house in town, stared up at the ceiling, planning out his next move.

Part of him was anxious to just get on out of town and find the gold before word got out about the murder, but he couldn't risk that. If he knew anything about the local law, the last thing anyone would suspect would be for the killer to actually stay in town. Odds were, once the body was found most folk would suspect he'd be long gone, wanting to put as much distance as possible between the law and himself.

Dane wasn't most folk, though.

If there was one thing he'd learned at an early age, it was that the best way to keep ahead of everyone was to never do what was expected. If someone thought that he was guilty about something, Dane had learned to turn that right around and accuse the accuser. That way, before anyone could pass judgment on him, they'd first have to figure out where the truth was coming from – and that usually gave Dane the time he needed to figure out his next move and get heading in that direction.

So, rather than head out of town, Dane knew he had to stick around – at least long enough to take care of the sheriff and the boy.

After that, he could take his time and take back the stolen gold.

Chapter Ten

The moment Johnny and Peter arrived at Etta's, the front door flew open and she came rushing out.

Dawn was just breaking and Johnny couldn't deny that the morning light washing over her face seemed to melt her years away. She was definitely an appealing woman but, at the moment, he had far more important things to deal with than thoughts of romance.

There was the matter of a killer who might well be looking to take care of Peter, the only witness to the man's crime.

Johnny helped Peter dismount and when Etta saw her son limping, she let out a cry and said, "What's wrong? What did you do to yourself, Peter?"

The young man winced as he allowed himself to put his weight on Johnny, who headed towards the house.

"Boy and I took a tumble in the woods," Johnny said, careful to keep his tone light. "Nothing serious. When we passed through town to come here, I had Wilfred get word to Doc Watts to come on out and take a look when he had the time."

Etta shook her head, glaring at Peter.

"Do you have any idea," she said, and Johnny heard the fear in her voice, "what you been putting me through, Peter? What in the world was you thinking, running off like that? Never you mind. You wasn't thinking, were you?"

The sheriff saw Peter's face heat up and he went over to Etta, placing a hand gently on her shoulder.

"Tell you what, Miss Etta – why don't we get you both inside and then you can tear into the boy as much as you like. Right now, though, I reckon he'd like to get out of those muddy clothes and maybe get something warm into him."

Peter shot Johnny a grateful look.

***

Half an hour later, after Peter got into some clean clothes and Etta had prepared some hot tea for everyone, Johnny decided that there was no point in putting off telling Etta what she needed to know.

After carefully setting down his cup, he cleared his throat and turned his attention to the lovely woman sitting beside him. Her blue eyes held his, and for some reason he felt suddenly nervous. He'd stared down men with guns aimed at him but right now, his heart beat faster than it ever had and he felt lightheaded.

Johnny took a deep breath.

"Miss Etta, there's something that you should maybe ought to know. When Peter was out there in the woods, he saw something he shouldn't have seen. Unfortunately, he saw a man get himself shot."

Etta's eyes widened in fright and she turned to Peter.

"Are you all right? Did you get hurt? Who was it who got shot?"

The boy shook his head and said, "I'm fine, Ma. I'm fine. Only reason I got hurt is I fell in the mud when the sheriff kept me from stepping into a bear trap."

"A bear trap?" she all but shrieked. "You could have lost your leg, Peter! I can't believe that you were so reckless that –
"

Johnny put his hand on her shoulder, then, and she turned to him, momentarily forgetting to stay panicked over what had happened.

"It's something that we can deal with later, Miss Etta. Right now, though, I'd like to focus on just what it is that I can do to keep Peter out of harm's way. Now, Doc Watts will be along to take a look at that leg and make sure it's fine. Once we get the go-ahead, I'm thinking that I'd like the two of you to stay with me. I got me plenty of room and I'd feel a whole lot better knowing that the two of you were in town, instead of out here all on your own."

Etta regarded Johnny with concern in her eyes.

"You think that the killer's going to be coming after Peter, don't you?"

"I think that might be one possibility, yes, ma'am," Johnny said, softly. "Of course, I could be wrong about that, but I'd really rather not take the chance."

***

Etta was frightened.

As she sat there, sipping on her now-cold tea, she tried to tell herself that everything was going to be all right. After all, she and Peter had already gone through so much before coming to this area, and they'd always managed to survive.

This time, though, things were different. This time, there was a killer involved.

As worried as she was, though, there was a part of her that was relieved that Sheriff Johnny Steele was helping them. From the moment she'd first come to town, there had been something about that tall, strong man that made her feel safe.

Etta knew she was comely, and she'd grown used to the looks that men gave her when their wives or girlfriends weren't around. There was a hunger in their gaze that made her uneasy.

When it came to Johnny Steele, though, all she saw in his eyes was concern and compassion. Although she hadn't told anyone in town about her past, she somehow felt as if the man instinctively knew what she'd been through and hadn't passed any kind of judgment on her. Knowing that he was there to protect her and Peter gave Etta a sense of security that she hadn't had in a very long time.

***

As Peter was gathering his dirty clothes for washing, he thought about what he hadn't told either his mother or Johnny.

He hadn't said anything about the gold that the man had been killed over.

Peter knew this was something that was important, something that he had to talk about. There was a part of him, though, that kept thinking about his life with his mother and how they were always just barely making enough to keep going. If he could get his hands on that gold, though, things would change. Everything would change.

The problem was he didn't have the slightest idea where the dead man might have hidden the gold – and even if he did, how would he even get it? The best thing for him to do would be to go to the sheriff and tell him everything that he'd overheard, yet, he couldn't get past the idea that if he could ever find that gold, he and his mother could finally have the life he knew she deserved ...

Chapter Eleven

Dane thought about the stolen gold.

He also thought about the other members of the gang – the ones he had left behind when he'd gone looking for Coy. Of course, they'd wanted to come with him but he'd made them stay in the cabin, about twenty miles outside of town. At the time, he'd told them the best way to track Coy had been to operate with as few men as possible, reducing the risk of Coy catching on too soon and going to ground.

Of course, that wasn't the real reason.

The real reason came down to greed. While Dane didn't mind splitting the ill-gotten gains he and the gang came across, he thought that he should be getting a little larger piece of the pie. After all, he was the man who had brought these people together, taught them how to keep the law from finding them, showed them how to stage a robbery so there was less chance of getting shot. It was only right that he took the lion's share of the loot.

Naturally, he never would have said that out loud to any of the gang; criminals tended to get upset if they thought someone was holding out on them. But, if Dane happened to get to the gold before they did, and he also just happened to take the gold for himself and put it somewhere for safekeeping and tell the others that he hadn't found it – well, who could blame him for that?

Of course, there were two problems at the moment – the sheriff and the boy.

It was possible that Dane could just get out of town, grab the rest of the gang and go looking for the gold together and then move on. He knew that might actually be the smart thing to do.

Sometimes, though, the smart thing wasn't the best idea.

After all, what if he found all the gold on his own and instead of just taking a little extra for himself, he simply kept the location of the gold hidden and went back to the gang and told them that Coy must have hidden it far away?

In order to do that, though, he had to make sure he could stick around long enough to go searching for the gold – and that meant the boy and the lawman had to be taken care of.

***

While Etta was with Peter in his room, Johnny took the time to look around their home.

It was in poor condition, he saw, but it was clean. Obviously, Etta took great pride in maintaining things but he saw some of the roof had water damage and that two of the windows were cracked.

Plus, the farmhouse was too secluded; the sheriff was all too aware of the way that criminals thought. Their first instinct was always to make sure they kept their identities hidden. Peter had seen the killer and it was more than likely the killer had seen him.

Johnny knew he was definitely doing the right thing in bringing them back to his place. They'd be in town and they'd definitely be safer. He wondered if that was the only reason he was doing this, though.

When he thought about Miss Etta – the way she looked, the way she cared about her child – it touched something in him. It had been a long time since Johnny had ever thought about any kind of life other than being a lawman, but things were changing.

Then again, he knew he couldn't pursue Miss Etta. It wouldn't be fair to her and it wouldn't be fair to Peter. The boy obviously could have used having a man in his life, but being the sheriff was a dangerous job. At any moment, he could fall victim to an accident while trying to help out one of the townspeople – or he might find himself in the woods with a bullet in him, like the poor soul he'd found at the beginning of this incident.

No, it was best to put any of those kinds of thoughts out of his mind and concentrate on just keeping Miss Etta and her boy safe.

***

As Etta packed some clothing, she found herself wondering about the sheriff. Everything about him spoke of strength, but mixed in with that strength was kindness. Where did that come from? The men in her past who had been strong had never shown any kindness towards her – especially Peter's father.

Memories of that night came back, as they often did. The door to her room being flung open, the drunken soldier staggering in. She'd called out, tried to keep him off of her. It hadn't worked. No one had answered her cries, no one had come rushing in to pull him off of her.

She looked down at her shaking hands.

Every time Peter asked her about his father, she found herself reliving that night, going back in time to when her life had changed forever. Of course, she also thought about the miracle that had come out of that awful incident – the boy who she loved with all her heart.

Etta knew some people would have said that Peter was the product of some bad seed and that he would never amount to anything. Those people were wrong. They hadn't seen the wonder and the innocence in his eyes when he was young, when she held him in her arms and he'd given her a gentle smile, giggling and laughing.

It didn't matter who his father was, she knew – what mattered was who his mother was and how much he was loved.

For a brief moment, she wondered what it would be like to have a man like Johnny Steele in her life – to have someone like that be around Peter, to show him what it meant to have both strength and kindness.

"You're being silly, Etta," she told herself. "Someone like that wouldn't want nothing to do with someone like you."

She knew that was true – but she also knew she could still dream.

Chapter Twelve

Johnny opened the front door to Etta's house and let Doc Watts enter. The old physician kicked some mud off his boots outside, then entered, taking off his hat.

"Thanks for coming so quickly, Doc," Johnny said, shaking the older man's hand. "I hope I didn't pull you away from nothing important."

"Well, Maggie Reynolds was trying to get me to eat some of her meatloaf again but after the last time I had some, I decided I'd rather head over to you and see what's going on. Go ahead and fill me in."

Johnny led Doc Watts over to the kitchen table, where Peter sat, his swollen ankle up on one of the chairs. The doctor sat down and examined the boy's leg for a few moments, frowning.

"Looks like you've got yourself a nasty sprain there, son. I'm going to move it a little and it's probably going to hurt."

He took Peter's foot in his hand and gently moved it from left to right, then from right to left. Johnny saw Peter wince in pain but the boy didn't cry out. That spoke volumes to the sheriff. He understood what it was like to feel pain and refuse to let it show.

"Well, the good news is that it's not broken. It's definitely just a sprain. Of course, that doesn't mean you can go out and sign up for a three-legged race any time soon, son. I'm going to want you to keep your weight off of it as much as possible and to try to keep it elevated."

Peter nodded. His face was pale and when he spoke, his voice was a little shaky.

"Yes, sir," he said. "I can do that."

"So, you think the boy might be good enough to travel back to my place, Doc?"

"I don't see why not."

Doc Watts stood up, then, and Johnny went over to him, putting his hand on his shoulder and said, "Mind if you and I step aside for a minute, Doc?"

"Not at all, Sheriff. What's on your mind?"

Johnny went outside and said, "I was just wondering, Doc, if you've noticed anyone new around town these past couple of days. I'm thinking there might be a stranger or two around here that I might be interested in."

The older man frowned, thinking, and finally said, "Well, I know there's a couple of families heading west that showed up about a week ago. They're waiting on a couple of other folk to join up with them – and there's just the usual straggler or two showing up in town for a couple of days. What's on your mind?"

Johnny sighed. "Well, I got me a body out in the woods here with a bullet in it. I'm going to send Wilfred out with some of the boys to bring the body into town. When I came across it, the storm was pretty fierce and I was really more concerned about finding the boy here than dealing with the body."

Doc Watts gave Johnny a searching look and said, "I take it you don't think the boy had anything to do with the killing?"

Johnny shook his head.

"No – but from what I can tell, the boy saw the killing take place, and that's not good. I'd appreciate it if you'd keep what

I told you to yourself, Doc. I don't want whoever's out there to know what it is that I know."

"Of course, Sheriff," the doctor said. "Naturally, I won't be mentioning that the boy and his mama are staying with you, either."

"Appreciate that."

Doc Watts started down the porch steps, then turned around and said, a mischievous glint in his brown eyes, "You know, Johnny, I don't think I've ever seen you act this way around a boy and his mother. Of course, Miss Etta is definitely a lovely young lady and I can't say as I blame you for wanting to keep her close – and the boy, too, of course."

"It ain't like that, Doc," Johnny said, but he felt his face growing hot.

The old man laughed, shaking his head. "You know, Johnny, I hear the words but somehow, they just don't ring true."

***

Peter sat on the edge of his bed, wincing as he carefully pulled his boot loosely over his swollen foot.

He was glad that he and his mother were going to stay with the sheriff. Although Peter tried to tell himself that he could handle any trouble that came along, he knew that wasn't the case. He'd just seen a man get shot and there was no doubt in his mind that the killer wouldn't hesitate to put a bullet in him, too.

Peter winced as he stood and he gritted his teeth. The last thing he wanted to do was have Sheriff Johnny think that he was some weak little baby who couldn't handle a little pain.

He was tough enough to deal with just about anything he had to deal with.

At that moment, there was a knock on his door and a moment later, the sheriff came in, looking at Peter with concern.

"Still hurts like the dickens, I reckon," Johnny said.

Peter shrugged, trying to act indifferent.

"I can live with it," he replied.

The sheriff let out a little laugh, then went over to him, placing his hand gently on Peter's shoulder. "If there's one thing that I've learned about pain, Peter, it's that it's only really bad when you keep it to yourself. The more pain you keep inside, the more you're going to find you're hurting."

"Yes, sir."

"Now, let me give you a hand to get you and your mother back to my place. After that, I've got some things that I need to take care of in town."

Chapter Thirteen

The journey to Johnny's house took about an hour. There were a couple of times when the sheriff could tell Peter's leg was hurting a little too much, so he forced Gunpowder to slow down.

The boy and Etta were in a makeshift wagon that Johnny occasionally used when getting supplies, and although he'd tried to make things as comfortable as possible, there was still a great deal of jouncing around. At one point, the wagon had hit a rut and Peter had cried out, causing the sheriff to stop and make sure his young charge was all right.

When they finally arrived at Johnny's home, he had Etta and Peter wait while he set up Peter's room. At least, that was how he had intended for things to work out. Within minutes, however, Etta had taken over and was making the guest bed up for her son, then heading into the kitchen to prepare some coffee and a quick meal.

Johnny attempted to stop her, telling her that she was a guest, but she simply gave him a long look and said, "Sheriff, we are not guests here. You are allowing us to use your home to keep my son safe and I'm not about to impose upon you. I've spent my entire life earning my keep and I'm not about to change that now."

Johnny had turned away before she could see the smile forming on his face.

After Peter got settled in, they sat down to some eggs and toast and coffee. Johnny took one sip of Etta's coffee and stared at her in amazement.

"How in the world did you manage to make your coffee taste like this?" he asked, unable to keep the surprise out of his voice. "Whenever I try to make coffee, it just sort of comes out like something out of Gunpowder's stall after I mucked it out."

She laughed and said, "Eggshells."

The sheriff raised his eyebrows. "Pardon me?" he asked.

"Eggshells, Sheriff. You add eggshells to the grounds. I thought everybody knew that."

"Not quite everybody," he admitted.

Peter, meanwhile, had been keeping quiet and Johnny gave him a concerned look.

"Everything all right, Peter? You hurting too much? You need to lie down?"

The boy shook his head. "I'm just taking everything in, Sheriff. This definitely wasn't something that I had planned to be doing."

"Well, don't you worry about a danged thing. We'll get everything straightened out and we'll get the two of you back home before you know it."

Johnny caught Etta looking at him and he said, "I know it's hard to leave your place, Miss Etta, but I promise you that I'll be doing everything I can to make the two of you comfortable."

Her eyes held his and when she spoke, there was a tenderness in her reply when she told him, "Sheriff, you've done more than enough. I'm sure that we'll be fine – and I thank you."

***

Etta found herself in a small room in the back of the sheriff's house, and as she made the bed and swept the floor, her thoughts kept returning to this man.

What in the world was it that could make a man who was surely exposed to violence because of his job somehow have such compassion and tenderness in him? Every man she had come across was nothing but sharp edges and pain. This man, though, was completely different – and that scared her.

Few men understood just how dangerous being around tenderness could be. When a woman grew up afraid to speak the wrong words, afraid to give the wrong look to a man, having someone there who wasn't looking to lash out was like a breath of fresh air.

The danger came from getting used to that, from thinking that could be a part of her life. She knew that wasn't the case. Things would change, go back to the way they'd been. She and Peter would be back in that house that was falling apart and Etta was certain that, sooner or later, Johnny would find the right woman to have by his side.

When she was young, she'd dreamt of meeting a man who would be there for her, protect her, care for her with a strength that came from love and not from aggression. In time, of course, those dreams had fallen by the wayside and she'd had to accept the harsh truth she was never going to have the kind of love in her life she'd once desperately wanted.

After all, love had proven to be nothing but a trap.

There had been a couple of men in her life, back when she was much younger. They hadn't really been men, though, just boys thinking they were men. They had said the right words, promised her all the things she wanted to hear, but all too soon, they'd shown her there was nothing to them other than words, and the future they'd been talking about was nothing more than an attempt to get something from her they wanted in a darkened bedroom.

So, she kept telling herself that even though Sheriff Johnny Steele might seem to be different from other men, the hard truth was she was not the kind of woman that he'd want in his life.

There was an edge to her that was never going to soften. Life had seen to that. After she'd had all of her dreams taken away and destroyed, she'd built up walls – and despite the fact that she wanted to take them down, she couldn't afford to.

For Peter's sake, though, she wished there was someone out there who would manage to get through all of her armor and take her and her son into his life – but she knew better than to allow herself that kind of dream.

It was better to deal with reality, accept her lot in life, and just keep working on providing the best possible life for her and her son.

Chapter Fourteen

After making sure that Peter and Etta were safe in his house, Johnny rode across town to the sheriff's office. When he got there, he saw that Wilfred was already preparing to head on out.

"Going somewhere, Wilfred?" Johnny asked, watching as his deputy grabbed his hat and vest.

The heavyset man nodded. "Doc Watts came by and told me what's going on. The way I see it, only reason you'd have to set those two up in your place is to keep them safe – which means the sooner I bring that body in the woods back and find out who it is, the sooner we can go after whoever did the killing. I'm figuring the boy saw the killer?"

Johnny nodded, sitting down behind his desk, moving some papers off to the side.

"Yeah, he saw something – but it was too dark out for him to get a good look at the killer. The thing is, the killer mighta gotten a good look at him, which is why I have the boy and his mother staying with me. I need to keep a close eye on them."

Wilfred chuckled, shaking his head. Johnny frowned, looking at him.

"Something funny, Wilfred?"

"Well, I was just thinking that Miss Etta is a mighty winsome young woman, Johnny, and I reckon there's quite a few men in town who wouldn't mind being in a position to keeping a close eye on her."

"It ain't nothing like that, Deputy," Johnny said, firmly. "I'd be doing this with anyone that might be in danger. You know that."

"Oh, sure – sure. Definitely. For example, I'm sure if Midge Hatterfield found herself in danger, you'd be the first one to take her in to keep her safe."

"That ain't fair," Johnny protested, weakly. "Ain't no one in their right mind gonna take that woman in, no matter how much danger she might be in. That woman would try the patience of a saint with all the complaining she does about everything."

"All I know, Sheriff, is that you could do a lot worse than having a woman like Miss Etta in your life, you know."

"How about you stop playing matchmaker and go out and find me that body? It'll be off the main trail, heading west. You'll find broken branches where I charged through."

Wilfred snorted.

"Sheriff," he said, "when you hired me as your deputy, you knew I was the best darned tracker around. If you think you've got to give me directions to finding what I could probably find with my eyes closed, you are insulting me."

Johnny chuckled and told him, "Just go on out there and get back with the body as soon as possible. The sooner we find out who he is, the sooner we'll be tracking down the killer."

***

Etta knocked on the door to Peter's room and stuck her head inside. She found the young man sitting up in bed, pillows propped up behind him. He was reading a book that the sheriff had lent him.

"How are you feeling?" she asked, feeling his forehead to make sure he wasn't running a fever.

"Ankle still hurts," he admitted, shaking his head, "but it's not that bad. I reckon I'll be up and about in no time."

Etta sighed. "You need to keep resting, Peter. I know that you're always in a hurry to get things done and get on with your life but you need to just slow down. There's no telling how much damage you can do to yourself if you push yourself too far too fast."

She watched her son roll his eyes. "Ma, I know you love me and I know you're always looking out for me, but you gotta remember that I'm not a baby anymore. I'm almost a man and I can't go around being treated like a kid all the time."

"Just because you're getting older, young man," she said firmly, "don't you ever go thinking that you're not always going to be my baby. That happens to be a mother's job in life – to always look out for her children, to keep them safe and to make sure they always do the right thing."

She noticed, then, Peter looked away when she mentioned the last part.

"Uh-oh," she said.

Peter looked at her. "What?"

"You're keeping something from me, aren't you? There's something that you're not telling me."

"It's nothing," he said, but she could tell from the strain in his voice he was definitely not giving her the whole story.

"Well, whatever it is that you're keeping to yourself, I think you might be better off telling Sheriff Johnny what it is that you know. The man is doing everything he can to keep you and me safe and he deserves to know whatever it is that you're keeping from him."

Peter sighed and said, "I'm real tired, Ma. I think I'm going to take a nap. You know – get some rest, right?"

For a moment, Etta wanted to press the matter but in the end, she simply nodded and left the room.

***

To Peter's surprise, he actually did manage to fall asleep after his mother left.

Unfortunately, he found himself having a nightmare. He was back in the woods, running away from the killer, desperately trying to stay alive. It was night in his dream and as he ran through the woods, he tripped over a large stone, falling to the ground.

He rolled over onto his back just in time to see the shadowy figure of the killer standing over him. The full moon peeked out from behind the thick clouds overhead and all Peter could see was the glint of moonlight off the barrel of the revolver.

"Time to take care of some business," the killer said, cocking the gun.

Peter snapped awake, heart pounding, just as the door to his room opened and the sheriff walked in.

"Easy, son," Johnny said, going over to where Peter was lying in bed. "I reckon you're just having yourself a nightmare. It's okay. You're safe here."

Peter took several deep breaths, forcing himself to calm down.

"It – it was just a bad dream," the boy finally said.

"I just wanted to see how you were doing. I sent Wilfred out to bring back the body so that Doc Watts could fill out his death certificate stuff and I could try to get a handle on who it was out there and maybe why he was killed."

"I think I might know why he was killed," Peter told Johnny.

The sheriff looked surprised but moved a small chair over to the bed, and sat down in it.

"I'm listening."

"I heard something when I was out there. I heard something about some gold," Peter said. "I didn't hear nothing about where it was or anything but I think the man who got killed was going to tell where it was but the killer got spooked or something. I don't think he was gonna kill the man before the man told him where the gold was."

Johnny nodded.

"I figured it mighta been something like that," the sheriff said softly.

Peter looked surprised and he asked, "You figured that? How?"

"Son, it's been my experience that most people don't just go around killing without a reason. Most times, there's usually a girl involved or else someone was cheating at cards or stole something. The card cheating usually takes place in a saloon – kinda a spur of the moment thing. Same thing with the girl – usually catches someone in the act and the killer handles it on the spot. It's what we call a 'crime of passion.' But the killing in the woods usually is someone trying to get information from someone about something that's been stolen. The killer wants time to have a little talk with whoever it is they're gonna kill so that the person can tell them what they want to know."

Peter nodded, impressed with the sheriff's reasoning.

"I should have told you sooner," the boy said, softly.

Johnny gave him a compassionate look and shrugged. "Way I see it, all that matters is that you told me, Peter – otherwise you might be tempted to go out there looking for that gold yourself and that would have been pretty danged foolish, what with a killer out there looking for the same thing."

Chapter Fifteen

Wilfred had sent a messenger to the Sheriff's Office telling Johnny they'd found the body and he was bringing it back to Doc Watts' place. Johnny locked up the office and headed across town to the small clinic across from the saloon.

When Johnny arrived, the first thing he noticed was the smell. The weather had sped up the decomposition process of the body and he breathed through his open mouth to keep the odor at bay.

Wilfred and Doc Watts were in the back room and when Johnny walked in, Wilfred said, "It's Coy McDill."

Johnny took in that information. He didn't really know all that much about Coy – just that the man had always seemed friendly enough to him, although maybe a little too much on the religious side for the sheriff's taste. He'd seen the man around at various social events and when someone needed something done, Coy had been one of the local handymen who would help out.

"How long's Coy been around here?" Johnny asked. "I reckon he was here before I showed up."

"About five years," Doc Watts said. "I think he came from back east. Wasn't the kind of fella that went around giving out a whole lot of information about his past. Not that that's unusual, though. Most folk I know like to keep their past close to themselves."

Johnny nodded to Wilfred, then, and glanced at the door.

"Doc," he said, "mind if I borrow Wilfred here for a few minutes? Something I need to talk to him about."

"Be my guest."

Wilfred followed Johnny out and when the door closed behind them, he asked, "What's going on, Sheriff?"

"Peter heard Coy and the killer talking about gold."

The deputy closed his eyes, shaking his head.

"Tarnation," he muttered.

"Right. If there's gold involved in this, you can figure the killer's probably not going to leave until he gets his hands on it. You got anything you can give me that I can use?"

"Afraid not," Wilfred said. "I been looking into any new arrivals in town and coming up with nothing, Johnny. There's no one out there really looking suspicious."

"It figures," Johnny said. "I reckon before the killer caught up to Coy, he'd been keeping a low profile in the area, waiting for just the right moment to make his move. I guess you and me will just have to handle things nice and easy, not make anyone notice. The last thing we need around here is a bunch of people deciding they're going to go out on their own and look for some hidden gold or something."

"How's the boy doing?" Wilfred asked.

Johnny grinned. "He's a tough one, all right, but he's a good one, too. Him and his mom might have had some tough breaks but you can see he's not the kind of kid to let it get to him. I think he's going to be all right."

"How's Miss Etta doing?" the deputy asked, with a smile on his face.

Johnny sighed. "Wilfred, you just best get back with Doc and see if there's anything he can tell us that might lead us to the killer. You can play matchmaker some other time."

***

While Peter was sleeping and Johnny was doing his sheriff business, Etta decided to straighten up the house.

She did the dishes, swept the floors, and was in the process of doing some dusting when she found a framed photograph that had been placed behind an old vase.

Etta picked it up, curious. She hadn't seen many photographs in her life and she was surprised that Johnny had one. When she looked at it, though, she felt her heart start to sink.

It was a young woman – maybe a little bit younger than Etta. She was wearing a summer dress and she had light hair and seemed to be looking right into the camera and smiling. She was the kind of a girl who looked like she definitely came from the right side of the tracks and just the sight of her made Etta realize that any foolish dreams she'd been keeping about her and Sheriff Johnny were just that – dreams.

She didn't know who this girl was or what her relation to Johnny was but Etta knew that, no matter how hard she tried, she would never be able to measure up to this total stranger.

***

Dane was back in the saloon, back in the shadows, listening carefully to everything that was going on.

There was a buzz going through the saloon at the unexpected discovery of Coy McDill's body. He heard a couple of people talking about Coy working at the local church and doing odd jobs around town but nothing that really caught his attention.

So far, there was no talk of any eyewitnesses to the crime or anything like that, which was good. That meant that even if the boy had talked, he hadn't talked to anyone who would have spread the news around.

In all likelihood, the only person that the boy would have told would have been the local law.

If Coy had hidden the gold, it would have been somewhere that he spent a lot of time, and from what folks were saying, that was the church.

It had been a long time since he'd felt the need to pray, Dane decided, finishing his drink and standing, but it might be time to pay a visit to the House of God.

Chapter Sixteen

Peter was definitely on the mend and he found himself not wanting to stay confined to his bed, needing to get up and about and move around.

His mother was cleaning house and he needed some fresh air. He carefully hobbled outside and saw some logs to the side of the house that looked like they needed to be chopped.

It took him a few moments to position himself so that he could do the wood chopping without hurting himself but he eventually found just the right stance. It felt good to be doing something other than just lying around and before he knew it, he was working himself into a solid sweat.

He saw Johnny ride up on Gunpowder and the sheriff dismounted, coming over to him, smiling.

"Well, looks like someone's feeling better," Johnny said.

"Yes, sir. I couldn't stand just lying in that bed one minute more," Peter replied. "I was going crazy."

Johnny laughed. "I know what you mean, son. I'm the same way. Nothing's more frustrating to me than just sitting around when my body's telling me it wants to do things."

Peter set down the ax and asked, "Anything new to tell me?"

"Matter of fact, there is," Johnny said. "Wilfred found the body and brought it back to Doc Watts' place. Turns out the dead man is Coy McDill."

Peter thought about that for a moment, then nodded. "Yeah. I thought I heard the killer call him 'Coy' but I wasn't sure. Everything seemed to be happening so fast and everything."

"Yeah. That's to be expected. Anyway, now that we've got a name, we can try to piece together just what in the blazes is going on around here."

The boy frowned, then, and asked, "Do you think the killer might still be in town or something, Sheriff?"

Johnny nodded.

"It wouldn't surprise me a bit. Gold's involved and the way I see it, if a man's willing to kill someone for gold, he's probably not going to pack up his bags and move along until he's got what he came for."

"So what are you going to do?" Peter asked.

"Well, I know Coy spent a lot of time with Pastor Brandon at the church, doing odd jobs for the preacher. I reckon I might as well see if there's anything the man can tell us about Coy."

***

Johnny's plan had been to have a talk with Pastor Brandon and maybe get some idea of what Coy had been up to.

Unfortunately, after heading back into town, as he went past the saloon, the front doors swung open and two men came brawling out, landing in the dirt.

Johnny recognized the larger of the two men as Dave Forrest and the man he was fighting was Kevin Stone. As a crowd gathered to watch the entertainment, Johnny jumped down from Gunpowder and went rushing over to where the blows were being exchanged.

Pushing his way past the onlookers until he reached Dave, Johnny grabbed the man from behind and physically pulled him back a couple of yards. At the same time, he saw Kevin moving forward, as if to land a blow while Dave was being restrained but the sheriff swept out with his foot to the side, causing Kevin to fall to the ground.

"Enough!" Johnny bellowed. "Now, I don't know what's going on here and I don't much care. I'm the sheriff around here and you know that means that I gotta keep the peace. I can't keep that peace when I got two grown men acting like boys on a playground."

After a moment, Johnny relaxed his grip on Dave, keeping a close eye on Kevin.

Dave pushed himself away, glaring at Kevin and said, "He's the one started it, Johnny. He claimed he caught more fish last summer than anyone else and everyone around here knows darned well it was me."

The other man shook his head and said, "You ain't remembering it right and that's a fact. Everyone around here knows I caught nearly twice as much as anyone else."

They continued to argue until Johnny grabbed Dave by the back of the neck and squeezed firmly.

"Now, then, is it safe for me to assume that I can take a step back from whatever the tarnation it is that is going on here without you two going back at each other?" he asked, shaking his head. "It don't matter who caught what and when, neither one of you needs to be getting into a ruckus over it. You hear me?"

Both men reluctantly nodded.

"Yes, sir," Kevin said.

"Sorry, Johnny," Dave added.

As both men once again tried to explain just what it was that had gotten them both so riled up, Johnny held up a hand, shaking his head.

"I'm not interested in what the story is," he said. "I just want the two of you to act like grown men and not have me waste my time with you. Can you do that?"

Again, both men nodded.

Getting back onto Gunpowder, Johnny glanced at the setting sun and sighed. It was getting late and he might as well head back home, to where he knew Etta would have supper waiting for him.

***

"So," Peter said, that night while they ate some stew and beans, "you didn't get to talk to the pastor?"

Johnny shook his head.

"No. By the time I got those two fools to simmer down and everything, it was danged near suppertime and I came back home. I'll talk to Pastor Brandon tomorrow."

Etta had been quiet since Johnny had come home that night.

The entire time she'd been preparing supper, she couldn't get the photograph of the young woman out of her thoughts. Who was this woman? Why did Johnny have a photograph of her? Was she a relative of his? A sister? A cousin?

She wondered if the woman had been something more close than that – and if that was why Sheriff Johnny had never really shown any interest in any of the women in town.

Had he had his heart broken, possibly, and he didn't want to go through that pain again?

She suddenly became aware that Johnny was watching her intently and she felt herself blush.

"This stew is mighty good, Miss Etta. I reckon you didn't put eggshells in it, though."

She found herself smiling and shook her head.

"No eggshells, Sheriff. Just stew, that's all."

"Well, I can tell you that this stew is nothing like I've ever been able to make," he admitted. "Somehow, the flavor just isn't the same."

"That's because good cooking, Sheriff, requires a woman's touch. Haven't you ever had a woman cook for you before?"

The moment the words came out of her mouth, she saw a hurt look appear in his eyes and Etta wished that she could take them back. Whatever had happened in Johnny's past had hurt him a great deal and she felt bad at having opened what looked like an old wound.

Johnny cleared his throat, then, and said, shaking his head, "I've had women cook before, Miss Etta, but nothing compared to what you've done here."

Chapter Seventeen

Johnny was sitting on the front porch when the door opened behind him. The light from the half-moon showed Etta coming out, standing in the doorway.

"Is everything okay, Sheriff?" she asked, softly.

He nodded. "Everything's fine, Miss Etta. Just doing some thinking out here, that's all."

There was a pause and then, in a soft voice, she asked, "Mind if I join you? I reckon I could use some fresh air."

He found himself smiling and moved over to one side, allowing her to sit beside him.

For a few minutes, they just sat in silence and finally, she said, her voice shaking, "I don't mind telling you that I'm worried sick, Sheriff. If anything ever happened to Peter, I don't know what I'd do. That boy is my whole life."

Johnny nodded. "I know. I can see that. Don't you worry, though – that son of yours is tough but it's a good kind of tough. He's got strength in him but he ain't mean. You should be proud of the job you've done, raising him."

"I am – it's nice to hear those words, though. It makes me think that maybe I've been doing right by him."

"I'd say you're doing just fine by him, Miss Etta. I know it must have been hard on you."

"You have no idea, Sheriff. All I've ever wanted to do was protect that boy and now – well, knowing there's a killer out there who might be looking for him, it makes my blood run cold."

"Well, you don't have to worry about that while I'm around, Miss Etta. It's my job to do whatever I can to protect the people in this town and I can promise you that I'm very good at my job."

Johnny saw Etta looking at him and he watched her features soften into something like relief. He reached over and took her hand, giving it a gentle squeeze.

After a moment, she squeezed his hand back.

***

Peter was getting ready for bed when there was a knock on the door, and Johnny stuck his head inside.

"Just wanted to say good night to you, son," Johnny said.

The boy grinned.

"Thanks, Sheriff."

Johnny came in and sat down. "You know, I've been thinking, what with you and your ma staying here for a little while, how about you and her just call me 'Johnny?' You think you can do that?"

"Yes, Sher – yes, Johnny."

The sheriff laughed, shaking his head.

"I know it'll take time to get used to that but since we're all here under the same roof, I'd appreciate it if you just were less formal."

"Okay, Johnny," Peter said.

"That's better."

Johnny went to leave but before he reached the door, Peter called out.

"Can I ask you something, Johnny?"

"Sure," he said, going over to the chair and sitting down next to the bed. "What's on your mind?"

"Did you always want to be a sheriff?"

Johnny seemed to think about that. Peter watched him carefully, waiting. After a few moments, the man shook his head.

"No. No, I didn't. I reckon I just wanted to be a rancher with a family. That's all. I just wanted to have myself a little place of my own and live a nice quiet life."

"What made you become a sheriff, then?"

Johnny's face clouded over and when he finally spoke, there was a tightness in his voice.

"The previous sheriff here was a good friend of mine. We'd grown up together and I reckon we were probably as close as brothers. I came to visit him one day and I found out that he'd been killed. There was a bank robbery and he'd tried to stop it. That was the kind of man he was; he always felt like he had to do the right thing, no matter if it got him hurt or not. Next thing I knew, I found myself putting on the badge and going after the men who killed him."

Peter's eyes were wide and he asked, "Did you find them?"

Johnny nodded.

"I did – and I brought them in. Hardest thing I ever had to do, son. Hardest thing I ever had to do."

"Why?" the boy asked, confused. "What was so hard about that?"

"I had the man who'd killed my friend on the ground in front of me, my revolver aimed right at him. I knew all I had to do was just squeeze that trigger and Richard's death would be avenged. The thing is, I had a badge on. It meant something. It meant that I had to put my feelings aside and do what the law wanted me to do. So, I took a deep breath and slowly put the gun down."

"Wow," Peter said, softly.

"You'll find one of the hardest things do to, I'm afraid, is doing the right thing when there's a part of you that wants to do the wrong thing.," Johnny said, standing up. "Now, you go and get some sleep."

***

Etta screamed.

She snapped awake, sitting up in bed. A moment later, the door to her room burst open and she saw a figure rushing toward her. Before it reached her, she was out of bed, grabbing a candlestick in her hand like a weapon.

"Miss Etta," came a familiar voice. "It's me. It's Johnny."

Relief flooded out of her and she set the candlestick down, then quickly donned her robe, collapsing onto the edge of the bed.

"I'm sorry," she said, voice shaking. "Sometimes, I get these nightmares and – and when I wake up, for a minute, I don't know where I am."

She felt the bed's weight shift as Johnny sat down next to her. He put his arm around her and drew her towards him.

At first, she stiffened but just the solid strength of his presence made her feel secure, safe. The memory of the nightmare was already fading and she took a deep breath, forcing herself to relax.

"I'm okay now, Sheriff," she said, softly.

"I reckon you'd better start calling me 'Johnny,'" he replied. "I already went through this with Peter."

"I'm okay now, Johnny."

"That's better," he said, softly. "You just try and get some rest now, Miss Etta. I know that you're worried about what's going on out there, but Wilfred and I have things under control. First thing tomorrow, we're going to go and have a talk with Pastor Brandon and find out if he can tell us anything about Coy that'll let us find the man who killed him – and that'll keep you and Peter safe."

He rose, then, and when he did, Etta couldn't help but feel a wave of regret that he was no longer beside her, holding her.

CHAPTER EIGHTEEN

Dane saw the church down the road and he approached it cautiously.

From spending time in the saloon, he'd learned enough about Coy to figure out the man had gone soft. He'd gone and hooked up with the local pastor, doing handyman work in exchange for room and board.

That was good.

That told Dane that the gold was stashed somewhere – and it was probably somewhere close by. No doubt there was going to have come a time when Coy would have done something stupid like donate all his money to the church or some foolishness like that.

It wouldn't be the first time the outlaw had seen that happen.

Some men, it looked like, started to get cold feet when they found religion. They were fine when they were young – doing what they wanted to do and not caring about anything other than money and women and staying one step ahead of the law. But then, something changed in them and the next thing anyone knew, they were dropping to their knees and deciding it was time to repent.

Dane knew he was never going to be one of those men.

If there was one thing he'd learned in life, it was that everyone needed to take care of themselves, no matter what. There wasn't anyone else out there looking down on them and wanting to make sure they did the right thing.

As Dane got closer to the church, he recognized the sheriff's horse hitched up outside and that gave him pause. There was another horse, too, and the outlaw saw the heavyset deputy and Steele sitting on the front steps of the church, talking to an older man who had to be the local pastor.

Dane paused, then, moving to the side of the dirt path leading to the small building and thinking about his next move.

The last thing in the world he wanted to do right then was have the local law show any interest in him. That meant any talk he wanted to have with the pastor was going to have to wait.

It wasn't ideal, of course – but Dane was a patient man. He knew all he had to do was bide his time and things would eventually work out. Of course, he'd have to give things a helping hand – such as take care of the law and the boy – but things would definitely work out.

***

Johnny and Wilfred sat on the steps of the church, listening to Father Brandon talk about what he knew of Coy's past. He'd heard about the murder, of course, and he told Johnny that it didn't surprise him.

"Why's that?" the sheriff asked.

Father Brandon let out a sad sigh. When he spoke, there was soft regret in his voice.

"When Coy first came to me and started working, Sheriff, I knew the man came from a troubled background. I could see it in his eyes, in the way he viewed the world. He had a lot of bad in his past and I knew the only peace he was ever going to find was in the Lord.

"So, I hired him to do small jobs for me around the church and I talked to him," Father Brandon continued. "The only way to reach the soul of a man like Coy is to do it gently. You can't come right at that kind of man and make them feel bad about everything they've done. You have to let them know that the Lord understands them and knows everything about them – and that the only thing the Lord cares about is that they want to make themselves into better men."

"Did he ever talk about his past?" Johnny asked.

The pastor nodded. "A few times," he said, "but nothing in great detail. I knew that he'd been with a gang of sorts and that he'd done things he wasn't proud of. He told me that he'd left the gang when he started to feel bad about what he'd done."

"Did he ever talk about taking anything from the gang?"

Father Brandon slowly shook his head.

"He didn't say anything specifically," he admitted, "but it wouldn't surprise me. I'd seen that before. The men like Coy start to think about what lies ahead of them when their lives in this world end and they start to want to make things right with the Lord – so they usually leave their wickedness behind and set out to make their way on the right path. They sometimes think that they can take their ill-gotten gains and make good to the Lord with it."

"He ever do anything like that?" Johnny asked. "He ever try to make good with you, Father?"

The older man shook his head.

"No. Oh, he talked about it, but it was in the sense of something he wanted to do in the future. I'm not sure, but I think it might have required him to travel somewhere. It wasn't something he carried with him."

Johnny nodded, glancing at Wilfred. That made sense. If Coy had taken gold from an outlaw gang, he wouldn't be carting it around in town. He would have had to have hidden it somewhere.

"Can I see his room?" Johnny asked, standing up and stretching. "There might be something there that can tell us a little more about where he came from – and who might have decided to end his life."

**

Peter was in his room, reading the book that Johnny had lent him. It was a handbook made for people involved with the law and Johnny said that it had helped him when he was first starting out as the local lawman.

There was a knock at the door and a few seconds later, Johnny came into the room.

He looked tired and Peter watched him sit down next to the bed.

"How are you feeling?" Johnny asked.

Peter nodded, grinning, and said, "I feel almost like my old self, Johnny. I can walk around just about like normal."

"Good to hear. I notice you're reading that book. What do you think?"

Peter thought about that for a moment. "It's got a lot of good information in it, Johnny, but there's this whole chapter about family and stuff in there."

"Yeah. There is."

"It says that a lot of lawmen don't cotton to the idea of family because the job is dangerous and they might not be

95

around that much because of hunting down criminals and things like that."

Johnny sighed.

"Well, that's true. It's not the kind of life cut out for everyone."

"What about you?" Peter asked. "Is it the kind of life that's cut out for you?"

The sheriff looked like he was about to say something but he cleared his throat and shook his head. "We can talk about that another time. Right now, your mom wanted me to come in and tell you to wash up for dinner."

With that, Johnny left the room and Peter wondered just what it was that the man had been about to say to him.

Chapter Nineteen

"Johnny," Etta said, softly, when they were sitting down for supper, "is everything all right? You've hardly touched your food."

The lawman looked across the table at the young woman and he forced himself to smile, nodding. "Everything's fine, Miss Etta. It's fine. I was just thinking about a couple of things, that's all."

What Johnny didn't tell her was that he was upset that he and Wilfred hadn't really found anything useful at the church. There was very little in Coy's room that gave any information about the man's past. Johnny had been hoping to find some clue that might lead him to learning about the outlaw gang that Coy had been part of.

There was no doubt in Johnny's mind that whatever outlaw past Coy had been part of was what had led to the man's death. Without having any concrete idea of where Coy came from, though, it was going to be almost impossible to track down Coy's killer.

More importantly, though, when Father Brandon revealed that Coy hadn't shown any signs of spending any gold, that meant it was still around somewhere – and that meant the killer was probably still hanging around, too.

The trouble was, there were so many newcomers to the area every day that it was difficult to find one that might be the outlaw Johnny was looking for. He'd learned from experience that most outlaws didn't look like they were outlaws. They looked like ordinary people – until they found themselves cornered by the law.

"Maybe the killer just got scared and run off," Peter said, hopefully.

"Maybe," Johnny admitted.

He didn't think that was the case, though. That wasn't the way outlaws worked. The killer had gone to the trouble of tracking Coy down and he wasn't about to walk away empty-handed. He'd want to find whatever gold it was Coy had taken and Johnny knew when most outlaws got themselves bitten by the gold bug, they weren't about to just pack up and move along.

No – Johnny was certain the killer was still somewhere close by, and he wasn't going to rest until he knew Etta and Peter were safe.

***

Etta was sitting outside the house when she heard the door open. Without turning around, she sensed that Johnny was there and she moved over slightly, letting him sit down.

"It's cold out here, Miss Etta," he said, putting a blanket around her shoulders. "You should be inside."

She sighed, glancing up at the night sky.

"I just can't seem to get comfortable, Johnny. I know that you're doing everything you can to find out who killed Coy and I appreciate that. It's just that – well, I can't stop thinking about Peter being in danger and it's got me all tied up in knots."

The lawman sat down beside her and Etta resisted the urge to rest her head on his broad shoulder. Part of her desperately wanted to be comforted, but she knew it would only be an illusion.

She wasn't someone who got to have a man like Johnny Steele in her life.

"Don't you worry about that. If he's around, you can rest easy because I'm going to find him. Between me and Wilfred, there's no way that he's going to be able to stay hidden for long."

"I appreciate that, Johnny."

"You know, Peter's got a good head on his shoulders and that boy's got more gumption than most men I know. He's got himself a bright future ahead of him."

"Well, you got him reading that stuff about being a lawman," Etta said, and she heard the concern in her voice, "and I just don't know if that's what he needs to be putting in his head right now. It's a cold and hard world out there, Johnny, and the thought that he might be wanting to go out into it and go after the kind of people who killed Coy – it makes me sick to my stomach."

"The boy asked me about what I do," Johnny said, and he shook his head, "and I just thought I'd show him that it wasn't what he might think it was. Some folk look at being a sheriff as a kind of big deal, where they get to walk around with a badge on their chest and tell people what to do. I just wanted him to see that it wasn't like that. It was about having to do the right thing all the time and about keeping people safe – especially the people who couldn't stand up for themselves. I never reckoned that he'd take to it the way he has and I'm sorry if it's causing you any trouble."

Etta sighed and took a deep breath. "If there's one thing I've learned with that boy, Johnny, it's that when he gets something into that head of his, there's nothing me or anyone else can say that's going to change his mind about it."

***

Peter was reading the lawman's handbook when there was a knock at the door.

"Come in, Johnny," he called.

The sheriff came into the room and gave Peter a wide grin.

"How'd you know it was me and not your ma?" he asked.

"Footfalls," Peter said. "You have a lot heavier sound when you step on that board just outside the door."

Johnny laughed.

"Well, now, I reckon that you might be the first non-lawman I ever heard use the word 'footfalls' with me," he said, pulling up a chair and sitting down. "How are you feeling?"

"I'm just about as good as I've ever been," Peter said.

"That's good to hear. So, I was just having a talk with your mother and she's a little worried about you getting all excited and everything about being a lawman."

Peter sighed. When he'd first started talking to his mother about the book he was reading, he'd seen on her face that she didn't like to hear what he was saying. He understood. She wanted to keep him safe and she didn't understand that that wasn't something she could do.

He'd seen a man get killed. It was a world out there that no one was safe in.

"She doesn't understand," Peter said.

"What's that?"

"She doesn't understand that she can't protect me. No one can really protect anyone, can they? I mean, I know that you try to protect people the best way you can but even you can't protect everyone at the same time. It can't be done. There are bad people in the world and even though we might want them to go away, that ain't gonna happen. There are always going to be bad people and the best thing to do is make sure there are good people to stand in the way."

Johnny raised his eyebrows and when he spoke, Peter heard genuine respect in his voice.

"Son," he said, softly, "that's about the best way I've ever heard anyone talk about what it means to be the law around here. You understand exactly what it means."

"You think I'd be a good sheriff?" Peter asked.

Johnny thought for a moment. "I think you'd do a lot of good no matter what you decide. It ain't so much the job that makes a person good or bad, it's who they are when they get there. Being sheriff ... yeah. You'd be a good sheriff. You care about folks. That's the most important part of the job. But you gotta remember, you can take care of folks in a lot of ways. Wearing a badge is just one of 'em, and for some folks, it ain't always the best choice."

"You sorry you're the sheriff?" Peter asked.

Johnny thought about that, then finally said, "Only thing I'm sorry about sometimes is missing out on family."

The sadness in Johnny's eyes kept Peter from asking any more questions.

Chapter Twenty

In the morning, Johnny found Etta in the kitchen, preparing breakfast. She gave him a bright smile and he couldn't help but feel a warmth spread through him. Something about that woman just gave him a sense of contentment he hadn't felt in a long time.

"Wilfred and I are going to be heading back out to the woods where we found Coy," he told her. "I don't think we're going to find anything new but I always like to go back to where something happened, just in case something slipped past me the first time."

She let out a little laugh and said, "Johnny Steele, I've been watching you for these past few days and I reckon there isn't a whole lot that slips past you."

He chuckled, shaking his head. "You'd be surprised, Miss Etta. Anyway, since you and Peter are going to be staying here for a while longer, I believe, there are some things up in the attic you might want to go through. I've got some blankets up there, I think, and some other things you might want to go and look at. It might make you feel a little more comfortable here, making the place the way you want it."

Etta gave him a long, searching look. Johnny felt like there was something she wanted to say but after a moment, she just nodded.

"Well, thank you, Johnny. I'll go and see what you've got and we can go from there."

As she continued to cook breakfast, Johnny watched her and found himself thinking that something about this woman just seemed to fit perfectly with the house.

When he'd first moved into the old sheriff's house, Johnny had felt there was a kind of loneliness about the place that he couldn't shake. After a while, though, he grew used to it – but since the arrival of Etta and Peter, he discovered there was a part of him that didn't want things to go back to the way they'd been.

He wondered how he was going to feel once they were gone – and he decided he didn't even want to think about that.

***

After Johnny left, Etta went up into the attic and looked around.

She quickly found the blankets that Johnny had talked about, along with a couple of plates and a beautiful pewter candlestick holder that was ornately carved. While she was examining that, her eyes fell upon a box that had a framed photograph in it.

She lifted the photograph up and took it to the small attic window, to get a better look at it.

It was the same woman who was in the photograph downstairs.

Looking at the woman, Etta couldn't help but feel envious. The woman in the picture was smiling and there was a happiness to her that almost hurt to look at. Etta couldn't ever remember being as happy as this woman seemed to be.

That was the way things were, she knew. Some people seemed just to be born to be happy and to have lives that were filled with joy and laughter. Others found themselves trapped in lives that contained nothing but pain and worry and concern.

Who was this woman? Why did Johnny have pictures of her and why hadn't he ever mentioned her?

Etta sighed and put the picture back. Whoever she was, she was beautiful, and Etta knew she could never compare to someone like that.

***

Back at the sheriff's office, Johnny and Wilfred were preparing to go out to the woods when Father Brandon came in. He had a small satchel in his hand that he set down on Johnny's desk and said, "After you left, I remembered that Coy used to have this with him when he went out. It wasn't in his room but I found it in the basement, where he used to spend his prayer time. He said it was where he felt closest to the Lord."

Johnny opened the bag. He took out a bible, what looked like some kind of journal, and some letters. There was no address on the letters but the letters themselves were written by someone named Trevor.

"Do you have any idea who wrote these letters?" Johnny asked.

Pastor Brandon shook his head.

"I'm afraid not. There were things that Coy didn't want to discuss with me and I always felt it best to let them slide past. I always told myself that when the time was right, he'd tell me whatever it was he wanted to tell me – but he never had the chance."

"Well, Father, thank you for this. Wilfred and I will go through it and see if there isn't anything there that might help us find the man who killed him."

"I wish you success, Sheriff," the pastor said, nodding as he headed towards the door, "and I will say a prayer to keep you and the deputy safe. There's a lot of evil out there in the world and those who are doing the Lord's work place themselves in harm's way all the time."

After he was gone, Wilfred said, "I don't know how some people do that, Johnny."

"Do what?"

"Spend all that time thinking about the Lord and doing all that praying and stuff and then have to look at the world and see how bad everything is. I've seen some things, Johnny, that make me sometimes wonder how such evil could be out there."

Johnny sighed.

"We're living in a fallen world, Wilfred, and about the only thing we can do is try our best to make sure that we leave this world of ours a little better off than when we found it."

Chapter Twenty-One

That night, at the dinner table, Johnny told Etta and Peter about what Father Brandon had brought him. He told them that when he and Wilfred went out to where Coy's body had been found, they hadn't found anything new that might lead them to where the killer might have gone.

"There were some letters from someone named Trevor," Johnny said, "that we looked over. There wasn't a lot to go on. In one of the letters, Trevor mentioned Coy telling him that he was feeling poorly and he thought it might be getting close to his time."

"So it looks like he might have been wanting to make his peace with the Lord before he died," Etta said, softly. "Poor man. He didn't realize what was going to cause his death, though."

"Was there anything in the letters about the gold, Sheriff?" Peter asked.

Johnny shook his head. "No. Obviously, he must have stashed the gold somewhere, but he didn't leave any trail to where it might be. We're gonna go through the letters again, though, and see if we might have missed something."

Etta shivered and said, "I just hate the thought that someone out there who killed a man is still running around loose. That ain't right."

"Well, don't worry about it, Miss Etta. Wilfred and I are doing everything we can to find the person who killed Coy and when we do, you can bet we'll be putting that man behind bars and sending him up for trial."

"It can't be soon enough," Etta said, firmly.

***

That night, Etta sat by the fireplace, doing some knitting. Johnny came in from taking care of the horses for the night and went over to her.

He sat down in the chair close to the fire and gave her a smile.

"You know, when we was at supper, you said that you couldn't wait for us to find the person who killed Coy. I reckon you was saying that because you were missing being back at your home."

Etta looked up from her knitting and shook her head. "No. That's not what I meant. I just meant that the sooner that person was behind bars, the sooner I'd feel safe. This has nothing to do with me wanting to be back home, Johnny."

"That's good. I just know that you and the boy never intended to have to leave your home and stay with me for this long. It must be hard being away is all I meant."

Etta gave him a long look and said, "Johnny, if there's one thing that I've learned in life, it's that a home ain't a building or a ranch or anything like that. A home is where a person feels safe and secure and knows that, no matter what comes along, they got themselves a place where ain't nothing going to hurt them – and sometimes a home ain't even a place, I reckon. Sometimes a home is just how you feel about someone."

***

That night, Johnny lay in bed, unable to get to sleep.

He kept thinking about Etta and Peter, what it felt like to have them in the house when he came home at night. Before they'd come along, coming home from work at night meant coming back to an empty house, making a meal out of whatever was around, and then just reading a little bit of the Bible and crawling into bed.

Now, however, he was coming home to a home-cooked meal and some conversation and just being around people that he felt a connection to.

He had to be careful, though. The last thing he needed was to start getting any ideas in his head. After all, they were only going to be staying with him until he found Coy's killer. After that, they'd be back in their own home and he'd be back to living a lonely life by himself.

He tossed to one side, slamming down his pillow, trying to get comfortable, trying to simply relax and let sleep come.

Impossible.

When he closed his eyes, he saw Etta sitting by the fire, knitting, and telling him that sometimes a home ain't even a place – that it was just about how you felt about someone.

Like it or not, he realized, he was beginning to think that Etta and Peter just might be his home – but he was a lawman and he knew that was something he just couldn't have.

Chapter Twenty-Two

"You okay, Sheriff?" Wilfred asked, the next day when they were at the office. "You look like you went two rounds with a grizzly bear."

Johnny yawned, rubbing his eyes.

"I reckon I didn't get enough sleep," he admitted. "Had myself a hard time drifting off. I kept thinking about the case, about what we're missing."

The two men were at their desks, going over the letters Trevor had written to Coy. One of the letters had Trevor promising Coy that he was never going to reveal the dead man's secret.

"What secret do you reckon he was talking about, Johnny?" Wilfred asked.

"It could be the secret of where the money is hidden," the sheriff said, "or it could be some other secret. I reckon we won't know that until we find out where Trevor is. I just wish we had some idea of where Coy came from. No one we've talked to has any idea about his past, about where he came from."

Wilfred shrugged and said, "Lot of people don't like to talk about their past, Sheriff. Heck, you and I been together for years, and neither one of us knows a whole lot about the other, right? That's just the way most people are."

Johnny thought about that and realized his deputy was right. In all the time that he'd known Wilfred, not much had been discussed about either of their pasts. For Johnny, he didn't like thinking too much about the past and he reckoned the same thing was true with Wilfred.

"Well, I guess we're just going to have to keep digging," he finally said, "until we find something that will lead us to the killer."

***

Etta was hanging out the wash while Johnny was at the office and she was softly humming to herself.

As much as she hated to admit it, she was finding it very easy to just let herself slip into thinking that she and Peter had a future with Johnny. Whenever she caught herself doing that, though, she'd force herself to face the hard truth – that this was only a temporary thing and sooner or later, she was going to have to give up this dream and return to where she came from.

For her part, even though it was going to hurt, she knew she'd be okay. It was going to be difficult on Peter, though.

It was easy to see that the boy was beginning to worship Johnny. He followed him around the moment the man came home from work, talking about the lawman's handbook he was reading and asking all kinds of questions about what it was like to be sheriff and how did he know so much and did he think that Peter would ever be able to become a sheriff like he was?

Etta found her eyes beginning to water and she took a deep breath, shaking her head.

She didn't want to think about what was coming in the future. For the moment, she just wanted to think about where she and Peter were right now – in a place that was beginning to feel an awful lot like a home.

***

When Johnny came home that night, he found Peter sitting on the front steps, waiting for him. The boy was bundled up in his coat, and the minute Johnny dismounted from Gunpowder, Peter went rushing over to him and said, "I just finished reading about outlaws and where they keep their loot, Johnny."

The lawman found himself grinning and said, "Well, you can tell me all about when we get inside. What in tarnation you doing out there in the cold, boy? You trying to catch yourself pneumonia?"

They went into the house. The moment Johnny entered, he smelled the savory aroma of rabbit stew and he found his mouth watering. He went into the kitchen, where Etta was getting out some bowls for the stew and he gave her a warm smile.

"Miss Etta, I gotta tell you – at the end of a day, coming home to the smell of your cooking does a man's heart good. This is something I could definitely get used to."

She smiled, shaking her head and said, "Don't you give me none of your flattery, Johnny Steele. I bet you'd say the same thing to Wilfred if the man knew how to cook."

Johnny burst out laughing, suddenly thinking of his deputy wearing an apron and standing over a stove.

"Well, now, I don't reckon I'd go that far, Miss Etta. Wilfred's as fine a deputy as any lawman could want but I've already tasted some of his cooking and I think I'd rather eat some of Gunpowder's feed, to be honest."

She giggled at that and said, "Wash up, then, and we'll eat."

***

After supper, Johnny and Etta were in the kitchen, washing and drying the dishes. At first, Etta had tried to keep Johnny from helping her but he'd told her that with the way she prepared those delicious meals, the only way he'd feel good about having her cook would be if she let him help clean up.

"I used to do it for my ma," he said, "and old habits die hard."

Etta washed the dishes and Johnny dried them. After a few moments, Etta said, in a soft voice, "I don't know if you noticed, Johnny, but that son of mine has definitely taken a shine to you. I'm pretty sure that if you told him that you could fly to the moon, I reckon he'd believe you."

Johnny chuckled. "Well, that boy's got a good head on his shoulders – and he's got a good instinct when it comes to understanding what it means to be a lawman. He's always got his nose buried in that book and he's always asking questions, which is good. Tell you the truth, I'm mighty fond of that son of yours."

"I hate the idea of him being a lawman, Johnny. No offense to you, of course, but if anything ever happened to him, I just know I wouldn't be able to handle it."

"He's young right now and he's just curious about a lot of things, I reckon. Give him enough time and I'm sure he'll get over it."

"I hope you're right."

"I know I am," Johnny said, then added, after a moment, "You know, that boy of yours is not the only one around here that I'm fond of."

Etta stopped washing the plate she held but she didn't look at Johnny. After a moment, she turned to him and said, "It's getting late. I reckon we'd better just hurry up and finish this and get some sleep."

Chapter Twenty-Three

Johnny, sitting at his desk in the jail, kept looking through the letters Coy had received from Trevor and studied the journal the man had kept. One thing that had amazed the sheriff was the way Coy wrote. It was almost poetic at times and that didn't fit in with the man Johnny had known.

Of course, one thing he'd learned as a lawman was that people sometimes were definitely not what they appeared to be.

He was broken out of his thoughts when the door opened and a tall, well-dressed man walked in. He had blonde hair and the bluest eyes Johnny had ever seen. He stood in the doorway for a moment, looking around, then settled his gaze on Johnny.

"Sheriff Steele?" the man asked, closing the door and approaching Johnny, hand outstretched.

Johnny rose and nodded. He shook the man's hand, noticing the grip was firm without trying to prove a point.

"Yes, sir. Can I help you?"

"I surely hope so. My name is Phil Anderson and I'm an insurance investigator currently working with the Pinkerton Detective Agency."

Over at his desk, Wilfred let out a low whistle. Johnny glanced over and was surprised to see a look of total admiration on his deputy's face.

"Wilfred Stander," Wilfred said, standing up and going over to shake Anderson's hand. "I been reading all about you fellas over at Pinkerton. You got yourselves quite a reputation."

Anderson laughed and told the deputy, "You'd better not believe everything you read in the papers, I'm afraid. Some of those newsboys want to make our lives out to be a lot more exciting than they actually are."

Johnny cleared his throat.

"So," he said, "what can I do for you, Detective?"

"First, you can call me 'Phil.' After that, I was hoping you might be able to help me figure out some stuff about a man that was shot – fella named Coy McDill."

Johnny and Wilfred exchanged looks.

"How'd you hear about that?" the sheriff asked.

Phil chuckled. "News travels faster than you think sometimes. Only reason anything came across my desk is because we've been looking for Coy McDill for quite some time."

"Why's that?"

"Coy McDill, once upon a time, was a part of Dane Kansas' gang. There was a gold robbery from a Wells Fargo stagecoach about five years ago. Two guards were killed and Dane and his boys got away with over a hundred thousand dollars in gold."

When Johnny heard the name "Dane Kansas," a cold chill went through him. He glanced over at Wilfred and saw the deputy watching him intently.

"I take it you've heard of Dane Kansas, Sheriff Steele?" Phil asked.

Johnny slowly nodded.

"Yeah. He killed the former sheriff – the man who was my best friend."

***

Etta swept the front porch of Johnny's house and took a deep breath.

She was tired. Sleep hadn't come to her easily the night before – not after the conversation she'd had with Johnny.

Etta wasn't sure about where she stood with Johnny. It seemed as if the man might be interested in her in a way that was definitely not unwelcome. The problem was that he didn't know her past, didn't know the truth about Peter and who the boy's father was.

The thought of having to tell him didn't sit well with her – and the thought that Peter would find out what she'd been keeping from him was enough to make her shudder.

At the same time, though, the idea that she might finally find a place in the world where she felt safe and loved – that was almost appealing enough to make her forget about everything else. Unfortunately, Etta had learned many of life's hardest lessons and one of those was that some people, through no fault of their own, were just not meant to find lasting happiness.

When she finished sweeping the porch, she went inside the house that she knew was never going to be her home.

***

"What can you tell us about Dane Kansas?" Johnny asked, pouring Phil a cup of coffee and bringing it over to the man sitting at his desk, going through Coy's letters and journal.

Phil took a sip of coffee and then raised his eyebrows, smiling. "Sheriff, you might be the first lawman I ever met who knows how to make a decent cup of coffee."

Johnny chuckled and said, "I learned it from a houseguest of mine."

Phil set the cup down and took a deep breath.

"All right – Dane Kansas. Well, obviously, everyone in the law enforcement world knows about old Dane. The man has one of the largest outlaw gangs out there and he's about as ruthless and deadly as they come. Personally, I'd rather find myself thrown into a pit of vipers than have to deal with Kansas."

Wilfred spoke up and asked, "Anyone have any idea what Dane looks like? I read in the papers that he's a master of disguise."

"Well, I don't know about that," Phil admitted, "but about the only people who know what the man looks like are the folks who work for him. Anyone else who's seen Dane has wound up dead."

Johnny nodded. "That sounds about right. Before I became the law around here, the previous sheriff was looking into a train robbery a few towns over. Word was that Dane Kansas and his boys were behind it and he thought he'd do some digging. Turns out the only thing being dug was his grave after he got killed."

"Dane Kansas?" Phil asked, softly, frowning.

Johnny nodded. "We think so. No witnesses, of course, but it makes sense. He must've gotten close enough to make Dane nervous and that meant he had to be taken care of."

"If we could only get our hands on one person who could tell us just who in tarnation this Dane Kansas is – one person who could help us come up with a sketch that could get passed around to every jail and police station in the country, we could finally put that animal behind bars."

Johnny shot Wilfred a warning look and slowly shook his head.

**

After Phil had left to head to the rooming house he was staying at, the deputy looked across the room at Johnny and said, "Any reason you didn't want me to tell the Pinkerton man about Peter maybe having seen Dane?"

"Right now, Wilfred, I want that information kept quiet. For one thing, Peter didn't actually get a good look at the man but I don't want the word to get out that might get back to Kansas. We know that the outlaw don't like loose ends – and I'll be danged if that boy is going to be a target for Dane Kansas more than he already might be."

"Sheriff, if Phil Anderson's right and we're dealing with Dane Kansas, that means the outlaw might already be in town, right?"

"Yeah. That's what it means."

"But we ain't got no idea what the man even looks like, so how in thunder and lightning we gonna find him?"

Johnny thought about that for a few moments, then said, softly, "I reckon I'm not sure yet, but I just might have me the beginning of a plan. Wilfred."

Chapter Twenty-Three

It was at supper that night that Johnny mentioned Phil Anderson's arrival in town. He took a sip of water, set the glass down carefully, and said, "So, Wilfred and I had ourselves an interesting visitor today."

He saw Peter immediately look up, and Etta tilted her head to one side, watching him carefully.

"Who was it?" she asked.

"Fella named Phil Anderson. Turns out that he works for the Pinkerton Detective Agency."

Hearing the words "Pinkerton Detective Agency" practically had Peter jumping out of his seat and the boy said, "Pinkerton? They're legendary! They're like the smartest detectives in the world, Johnny."

The sheriff chuckled and said, "Well, I don't know about that. Phil Anderson said the newspapers like to exaggerate things a little."

"Why was he in town, Johnny?" Etta asked, and he heard the tightness in her voice.

"Well," he said, slowly, "it turns out the man's interested in Coy's murder and wanted to see what information we had."

"Why in the world would a fancy detective agency care about someone like Coy?" she pressed. "Seems to me that don't make a whole lot of sense."

Johnny took a deep breath. "Well, it's not for certain but it's possible that Coy might have been part of Dane Kansas' gang."

Etta's eyes widened and she said, "The outlaw?"

"That's – scary," Peter muttered, shaking his head.

"Now, there's no need to get ourselves all worked up over what might turn out to be nothing," Johnny told them. "First of all, we don't know for sure that Dane Kansas and Coy even knew each other. There was nothing in any of Coy's belongings that mentioned Dane by name. Even if it's true, though, Dane is probably long gone after killing Coy. For all we know, the outlaw already found the gold or whatever it was that he was looking for and he's moved on. He'd have to be a danged fool to stick around when he might wind up being caught – and if there's anything we know about Dane Kansas, it's that the man ain't no fool."

"Papers said he also don't let anyone live who might have seen him," Peter said. "I know that much."

"You didn't mention Peter to this Pinkerton man, did you, Johnny?"

The sheriff shook his head.

"No, ma'am. That's one thing you don't have to worry about. Me and Wilfred both decided that the less people who know about Peter, the better."

They ate for a few more minutes and then Peter said, "Can I go to work with you, Sheriff, and meet this man from Pinkerton?"

Johnny avoided looking at Etta as he said, "I reckon that might be arranged. He's going to be coming by in the morning to let me know if he found anything useful in Coy's letters and journal."

Peter's face glowed with excitement but Johnny kept his eyes set firmly on the stew they'd been eating, not wanting to see how Etta had taken the news.

***

"What in the world were you thinking, Johnny Steele?" Etta demanded, clearing away the dishes later on. "Why would you encourage him?"

"The boy's interested in law enforcement, that's all. I reckon just about any boy his age would want to meet someone from Pinkerton. They write books about those guys. It'll be fine – and maybe Phil can let him know that it's not all excitement and action. There are plenty of times when it's just like any other job out there."

"Other jobs don't have deadly outlaws hunting people down and killing them, Johnny."

"He's going to be with me and Wilfred and Phil, Miss Etta. I reckon between the three of us we can make sure that Peter stays pretty darned safe, you know."

She sighed, shaking her head. "Well, there's nothing I can say, is there? The boy's already looking forward to tomorrow and if I tried to take that away from him, he'd only wind up getting mad at me. I guess I'll just have to trust that you'll make sure nothing happens to him."

Johnny went over to where she stood at the table and turned her around to face him. At first she didn't want to look at him, but eventually she sighed and stared into his eyes.

"If I thought for one minute that anything could happen to Peter, you know I never would have said a word. He's going to be with us in the jail office and I really don't think that Dane Kansas would come within a thousand miles of any place that could put him behind bars. Peter will be fine."

Etta stared up at him and then slowly nodded.

"Fine, Johnny Steele – but I'm trusting you with my most important possession in this world. You'd best not let anything happen to him."

Johnny looked into her eyes, saw her concern and also saw her trust, and he said, in a soft, gentle voice, "Miss Etta, you can trust me with anything in the world because I would never do anything to hurt you and that boy of yours. Believe that."

***

Peter woke up in the middle of the night, suddenly alert.

He wasn't sure why had been awakened but he lay in bed, just listening.

After a moment, he heard a board creak outside the house. It sounded like it was one of the loose boards on the front porch.

The first thought that went through his mind was that Johnny was anxious about everything going on and had gone outside to do some thinking. It wasn't the first time that the sheriff had done that and Peter quickly put on his clothes and quietly went and opened the door to his room.

Moving with as much stealth as possible, he went to the front door and opened it. A blast of cold wind rushed in and he quickly stepped outside, closing the door behind him.

"Johnny?" he whispered. "You out here?"

Looking around, he saw no sign of the lawman and he went around to the side of the porch, where he'd heard the initial noise.

There was no one there.

Peter was about to go back inside when he saw a shape standing in the shadows of the trees a short distance from the house. His heart pounded. Although he couldn't make out any of the man's features, he had no doubt who it was.

Dane Kansas.

"Well, well, well – I reckon you and me got something to talk about, boy. I heard that you saw something you shouldn't have seen. I reckon I'm going to have to take care of that."

Peter turned to go rushing into the house, but he looked down and discovered the porch was gone and he was standing in a puddle of quicksand. When he tried to move, it was impossible.

There was a cold chuckle behind him.

"Where you going, boy? You and me got some business we need to take care of. I can't have someone like you running around telling people you seen me. I can't have that at all."

"I didn't see you," Peter whispered, shaking. "I didn't see anything."

"Now that's a shame, then, because I saw you, you see. I guess if I saw you, I just gotta assume you seen me – and you know I'm not the kind of man goes around leaving behind any loose ends."

A hand landed on his shoulder, then, and Peter cried out.

***

"Easy, son," Johnny said, sitting on the edge of the bed, "it's okay."

Peter's eyes were wide with terror and he sat up in bed, looking around. Confusion filled his features but after a few moments, he began to slowly relax.

"I – I was having a nightmare."

Johnny nodded and said, "I heard you moaning when I got up for a drink of water. Figured I'd better come in and make sure you was okay."

"I was having a nightmare about Dane Kansas."

"Makes sense. We was talking about him at supper and he's probably on your mind. You're okay now. Just a bad dream. Nothing to worry about."

Peter looked at him and there was no mistaking the fear in the boy's eyes.

"You reckon Dane Kansas is really still out there looking for me, Johnny?"

The sheriff thought about that for a long moment. The last thing in the world he wanted to do was lie to Peter but he also didn't want the youngster to be afraid to even go outside on his own.

"Son, I reckon if Dane Kansas is as smart as everyone seems to think he is, he's gonna know better than to mess with anyone that I'm sworn to protect."

Chapter Twenty-Four

In a small, wooden, one-room shack on the outskirts of town, Dane Kansas sat in one of two straight-backed chairs. A kerosene lamp burned on an overturned apple crate, providing the only light in the room. The wind blew loudly outside, finding the chinks between the old walls and sending a chill into the room.

Dane had stumbled across the place by accident years ago and kept its presence mostly to himself. The building looked to be an old trapper's cabin, but it had long been deserted when he'd come across it. In spite of all his comings and goings, all the young men he'd had in and out of his gang, he'd kept the shack a secret. Just in case. You never know when you're going to need a place to lay low, and doing so without any loose lips to give the hideout away was even more important.

Sometimes drastic action must be taken, however. Dane had weighed his options countless times since his encounter with Coy, and more importantly, with the boy. If he was going to make any progress, he would need help; there were too many steps, too much ground to cover. If he were to try it on his own, he may as well move into the cabin and settle in. With a few extra hands, though, things might move more smoothly.

He supposed that would require divvying up the gold at the end of the day, but then again – he grinned to himself – maybe it would only *imply* a divvying up. Plans change quickly, and he might need to keep this cabin secret again after things were taken care of. Two outlaws turning up dead when they were no longer useful wouldn't be anything new.

First, though, the gold. Without that, he may as well make plans on moving into the White House with old Rutherford Hayes himself. Plans were cheap.

Thankfully, he'd been able to track down the one young man he knew he could count on in a bind. Between him and a lucky break Dane had fallen into with a third man, they could make short work of things. Theoretically. It would depend on the young man sitting with him now and the older man in the rooming house in town. More people involved than he cared for, if he was being honest.

"You want me to do what?" the young man in the other chair said.

"You heard me," Dane said. "It shouldn't be anything too difficult for you. There are windows, doors. It's just like anywhere else. Pick a place and make an entrance."

Jake Miller was in his late twenties. He'd been by Dane's side in a number of schemes and proven his mettle each and every time. More importantly, he'd proven his loyalty. Without either of them ever mentioning it, Dane knew Jake fancied himself taking over the Kansas gang when Dane died or retired. That was fine with Dane; it made the young man easier to manipulate.

And besides, the kid had skills Dane had always been too impatient to develop, one of which was getting into locked buildings without breaking out the windows or kicking the door in.

"Oh it's got doors all right," Jake said, taking off his hat and running a hand through his hair. "The problem is, the ones in the back are all bars. I ain't saying I never spent a night in jail, but I can tell ya it's not something I enjoyed none too much."

Dane allowed himself a small grin. "Yeah, it comes with the territory, I'm afraid. Think about it this way, though, friend. Of all the places you could be breaking into, is there any less likely?"

Jake shook his head, a small smile playing at the corner of his mouth. "I reckon you got a point there."

"Besides," Dane continued, "it will be a quick job. I just need a few things that, for all we know, may not even be there."

"You don't know?"

"I have a strong feeling,' Dane said. "And to be honest, you best be hoping they are. If not, you'll be breaking into the sheriff's house next, and something tells me that won't sit well with the man."

"Breaking into his office will?"

Dane shrugged. "Call it a neutral territory. A man's home though ..." he sighed. "Let's not worry ourselves about that 'lessen we need to."

"So what am I after exactly?" Jake asked.

Dane smiled again. It was a good sign. The young man didn't need details about the process, only the goal. He trusted Dane with the rest of it.

"To be frank," Dane said, "I'm not entirely sure. If I were you, I'd keep an eye out for a journal, papers, possibly personal effects. Anything that the sheriff turned up out at the church. I planned on getting to the pastor first, but this Steele fellow is a wily as they say and beat me to it. Whatever he's got on Coy will either be out or easily found, so don't waste too much time rooting around. If you don't see anything in the first, let's say ... ten minutes, I'd wager the fella done took it home with him ... in which case, we got ourselves a new set of problems."

Jake rubbed his forehead. "Maybe papers, maybe books, maybe nothin'."

Dane looked the young man in the eye. "Maybe. Is that a problem?"

Jake looked at the dirt floor for a second, the ground pounded hard as rock after years of footsteps. "Don't reckon so," he said.

"Good," Dane replied. "And not to worry; you won't be on your own. I've got another fella in mind who should know just what we're after."

"Who's that?" Jake asked.

"Who I'm going to see next," Dane said, standing up. "Meet me back here in twenty-four hours and I reckon you'll find out for yourself."

***

The saloon wasn't in the town proper. In fact, it was barely in a village – if one could call it that – but Dane had no intention of spending any more time in the eyes of the regular folk than he needed to. It was impossible to keep track of all the folks who knew folks who might know the sheriff.

The man had been waiting for Dane when he'd arrived. A good sign. Ideally, Dane would've gotten there first, given himself a chance to settle back in a corner and keep an eye on his surroundings, but making the man wait, well that was just as good, he supposed. It showed Dane's authority, something he felt the current situation had begun to undermine.

"The kid's in," Dane had said, sitting down. "Now, I need to know what you've got. Don't make this a waste of everyone's time."

Detective Phil Anderson looked back across the table, his eyes calm, appraising. "You ain't much on patience, are ya?"

"Not when it comes to gold," Dane said, holding Anderson's gaze. "What've you found out?"

Anderson shrugged, took a drink of his beer, purposefully drawing the moment out. Dane could feel it, and he despised the man for it. "Steele don't have much as of yet. He's mostly speculatin'."

Dane gritted his teeth. "Let me ask you something," he said slowly. "Does Steele have any idea who I am?"

"Not that I know of. He knows your name, but other than stories, he didn't seem to have much by way of facts."

"So we agree then, that there's little reason I couldn't go in and do what you're doing myself and he'd never be the wiser. I suggest you remember who's running this gang and stop with the lollygagging."

A faint smile flashed across Anderson's face and he spoke again before Dane had a chance to reprimand him. "He's got what you were looking for. The journals. Some letters too. Seems to me that's what we need more'n anything. If Trevor and Coy hashed something out, it'll be in those."

"And where are they now?"

Anderson moved his head from side to side, shrugging a little. "If I had to guess, I'd say the office. I kept an eye on the place from across the street and didn't see Steele takin' nothing home, leastwise."

"All right," Dane said. "The plan stands then. I'll set things up with your partner; you'll plan to make a move within forty-eight hours."

"Anything in the meantime?"

Dane looked at Anderson. He didn't need the man, but it was better to put some space between himself and the sheriff if at all possible. Besides, if someone was going to get caught breaking into the office, he sure didn't want it to be him. Dane started to shake his head, then paused. "Actually yes. Keep your ears open about a boy. Maybe fifteen or so. There're rumors around that he knows something he shouldn't."

"You want to tell me any more than that? Can't very well go asking Steele if there's any boys in the town. I reckon I can see for myself there's a slew of 'em."

"No," Dane said. "Don't ask anything. Just pay attention. If the sheriff brings it up, do whatever a real detective would do."

"Hey, I'm real enough," Anderson said, grinning.

"Do whatever an honest detective would do then," Dane said, standing up.

Anderson raised his mug. "We're all crooked one way or another. Some just got bigger bends than the rest."

Dane thought about replying, but instead turned and headed back out into the windy night. In a few days, this could all be over. Just a few more days.

Chapter Twenty-Five

The next morning, Etta looked along the shelves in the general store. Johnny had left her some money, telling her to pick up whatever she needed as she saw fit. Initially, she'd assumed it was just his way of keeping her busy, trying to keep her mind off the fact that he and Peter were off on their adventure together, something that she'd worry about until she heard their steps at the door. But in some ways, it was funny, too. She felt like too much of a guest to impose on both his home and his bank account and wanted to take care of things as well as she could without causing too many waves for the man. In other ways, this felt exactly like what she should be doing. It was the feeling of home, of a family, that she'd longed for all her life.

At the same time, in the back of her mind, the dark thoughts lingered as always, telling her she was broken, damaged, not worthy of anything as good as a family all her own.

She walked down toward the barrels of flour and sugar, running through recipes in her mind, when the conversation between the store owner and another customer caught her ear.

She couldn't be sure at first, but the second time she heard 'Coy,' she knew it was the name and not the description. Etta worked her way closer to the two men who were leaning on the wooden counter at the front of the store.

"Now that ain't what I heard at all," the shopkeeper was saying. "You're right about the money, but word now is, it warn't no notes. It was all gold."

The customer across from him whistled. "Reckon that'd be a little easier to stash away."

The shopkeeper shrugged. "If stashin' is what you think they done with it. If I was a bettin' man, I'd say that gold's been long blown on booze and women. Lost at cards. Spent on nonsense. That's the problem with outlaws, they don't got enough sense to see something good when it's in front of it. Think there's always gonna be more around the corner."

Etta reached up and felt a bolt of cloth, not out of any interest in buying it, but in hopes the men would keep talking. *Gold?* She remembered hearing about the Wells-Fargo robbery, but back then, as now, she didn't allow herself much time for gossip. If it didn't relate to her or Peter, she tended to brush it out of her mind.

"Here's the thing, though," the man at the counter said. "If'n it's all gone, like you reckon, why come after Coy?"

The owner shrugged. "You're askin' the wrong question here. Before we can start wondering why the come after Coy, we gotta be askin' just who was Coy to begin with? I'm sure you heard the rumors same as me."

"Well yeah but … you know how it is. Rumors come pretty cheap around here. You really think he was tied up with all that?"

"I'd about reckon this proves he was. And it'd stand to reason he either knew where that gold is now, or he knows what happened to it."

"You don't think he coulda just crossed the wrong fella?"

"Doing what? That man's been a saint since he showed up. Father Brandon don't ask much about where folks come from to begin with, but the fact that Coy's been out there with him all that time, makes me think whatever come back to haunt him ain't nothing from around this town. He'd barely say hush to a dog, let alone get himself into the kind of trouble worth murdering over." He paused. "Ma'am? Can I help you with anything? I didn't mean to be jawin' the day away up here."

Startled, Etta felt her face redden. She'd hoped they hadn't noticed her, something she found herself hoping most places. She muttered a "no, thank you" quickly and tried to focus on the recipe in her mind.

"How's the boy?"

At first, she thought she'd misheard, but the lengthy silence in the store made her turn to the two men, both looking at her with expectant, though not unfriendly faces. "Beg your pardon?" she said.

"Your boy," the man at the counter said. "He was the one got hisself all turned around during that storm few days back, wasn't he?"

"Oh," Etta looked down. "Yes. Peter. I didn't realize that was local news." She glanced at the two men, feeling her cheeks redden.

"Gotta have something to talk about if I'm gonna stand here all day," the man said, smiling. "I'll tell ya what, that Sheriff Steele, he's the best thing happened to this town in a good while."

"Yes," Etta said, unsure where to look or even how to respond. "He was very helpful. Peter gave me such a fright."

"Ah," the man behind the counter pulled a stool across the wooden floor and sat down. "That's boys for ya. They get to be that age and you may as well just put a plate of food on the porch. Bout as reliable as barn cats." He laughed.

Etta smiled, in spite of herself. She knew that she and Peter weren't invisible in the town, but the idea that other people could be so familiar with what happened in their lives was a bit unnerving. The men seemed friendly enough, though. And if they knew so much about her life, they certainly weren't turning up their noses at the fact that Peter's father was nowhere to be found.

Nervous, but doing her best to accept the smiles of the two men, she spoke up. "You were talking about Coy ... McDill, right? I wasn't eavesdropping, of course, I just ..."

The owner waved a hand in the air. "We ain't got nothing worth eavesdropping on. You listen to this one too long you'll be so turned around you won't know which way is up. But, yeah. You know Coy?"

"No," Etta looked down. Were they implying something? "I just heard that ... well ... he was killed."

"You know about as much as anybody else, then," the man on her side of the counter said. He was a scrawny fellow, someone who ought to be out doing something, though manual labor didn't look like it would agree with his scant frame. "Everybody's opinion is welcome at this point. Till the sheriff comes out and tells us what happened, we may as well blame it on the spirits."

"Oh. Has Johnny ... I mean, the sheriff, figured it out already?" This was certainly news to her.

The man shrugged and the store owner took up the conversation. "Fella like him, he coulda figured it out from the get-go, but until he wants somebody to know, he ain't gonna breathe a word. That man's a steel trap."

An image of Peter's close encounter with just such a contraption flashed through Etta's mind, but she shook it away. "You seem to think highly of him."

The shop owner looked at her. "Listen, anybody that's been through what that man has and ain't done up and left people behind him, that's a heck of a fella in my book."

"Oh," Etta said. "Yes. I'd heard he was friends with the previous sheriff."

"Not to speak ill of the deceased," the man said, "but I reckon by that point, he about done expected it."

Etta furrowed her brow. "What do you mean?"

"Death's been following that man around for going on two decades now," the owner said, pushing his hat back. "Ole Johnny wasn't always the only Steele in town. He growed up here. Had folks, naturally, and a younger sister ..." he looked at the man across from him. "Theresa?"

"Twila."

"Twila," the owner said, turning back to Etta. "Lovely girl. A firecracker, but that's to be expected, I reckon, with an older brother like him. She was by his side constantly."

"What happened to her?" Etta asked, wondering if perhaps this was the mysterious woman in the photo.

"Scarlet fever," the man said. "This was ... oh nearly twenty years ago, I reckon. Ole Johnny was devastated. He was only about sixteen, seventeen when it happened. Shut up tight as a clam for a long time. I remember seeing him around, working odd jobs here and there. Felt terrible for him then, but little did we know he wasn't but just beginning his hard times."

Etta took a few steps closer, setting her basket on the wooden counter top.

"His folks died a few years later." He looked at his friend again. "Cholera?"

"Mountain fever is what they said got his ma," the man said, naming a disease that, as far as Etta knew, could mean a hundred different things. "His pa died in that wagon accident out east of town."

"That's right," the shop owner agreed. "I plum forgot about that. Terrible of me." He turned back to Etta. "Then, his older sister, Grace, and her child were lost to the fever, too." He shook his head. "To make a long story short, the good Lord saw fit to take all of the Steeles and leave Johnny on his own."

"How awful," Etta said.

"It don't get no better," the slim man at the counter said. "He had hisself a gal there for a time. You remember that?"

The owner nodded. "The Johnson girl." He looked at Etta again. "They ain't been around these parts for a long while. Her and Johnny was pretty sweet on each other though. Course, with the war coming up this way, Johnny felt it was his duty to take part. Promised to come back and marry his girl, settle down. He come back all right, something that I don't reckon most folks counted on. Smallpox had got her in the meantime though. Her family up and headed back east right after it happened. He didn't even find out till almost six months later."

Etta put a hand to her mouth. "That poor man."

The shopkeeper nodded again. "Yes, so, if you excuse my sayin', I sometimes wonder if Johnny was any too surprised when the sheriff got shot. Just another person he'd gotten close to."

The three of them looked at one another for a moment, unsure of how to continue the conversation.

"But that's why you gotta admire the man," the other customer finally spoke up. "You can't keep him down. No matter what happens, he always fights his way back."

"You got that right," the store owner said. "And if anybody's gonna get this Coy business straightened out, it'll be him. You can count on that."

Etta repeated the last few words to herself. It was something she'd been thinking about the man, if not overtly, at least in the back of her mind, though she hadn't admitted it until now, until hearing it said by someone else. If there was anyone she could count on, it was Sheriff Steele, Johnny.

She turned back to her shopping, wanting to hurry back to the house and begin dinner. What she'd learned wasn't something she'd ever bring up with Johnny, but it certainly gave her a lot to think about, and she needed time to sort it out in her mind.

Chapter Twenty-Six

Across town, Johnny Steele was trying to lay out a simple plan for his own small trio.

"I'll trust you on it," Wilfred said. "Always best to play it safe first. Just don't be surprised if the man is a little miffed at getting left out."

"I can deal with miffed," Johnny said. "But we got more important things to keep in mind at the moment." He motioned with his eyes toward Peter, who sat behind the desk, flipping through papers and investigating drawers. "Etta trusts me, and I trust you. When it comes to Anderson, Pinkerton or not, I don't know the man. That's all there is to it."

"Pinkertons are the best," Peter spoke up, indicating that his apparent focus on the tangible items of sheriffing wasn't total. "They never sleep. Or at least, that's their motto. I reckon they gotta at some point though." He toyed with a pair of cuffs that were sitting on the desk. "We gonna need these today?"

Johnny smiled. "Not if I can help it. But," he added, taking the cuffs from the boy, "it never hurts to be safe."

"What's our plan?" the boy asked, his eyes bright. "Walk the town? Do some interviews? Find clues?"

Johnny was relieved at the boy's excitement. Initially, he'd hoped to just introduce Peter to Wilfred and show him around the jail and office. If Anderson had been there, the youth could've met the detective too. But, given the opportunity of a day for just the three of them, Johnny wanted to look around a bit more without any extra eyes. Plus, no matter what Anderson might have told them so far, he thought to himself again, he just didn't know the detective yet.

"Some walking, yep. One interview. Hopefully lots of clues," Johnny said.

"Oh," Peter sounded a little disappointed. "No riding?"

Johnny laughed. "Not today. We aren't going far enough to make it worth the horses' time. Besides, folks always see horses and think 'posse.' We're just folks out for a stroll."

Wilfred stood up and cracked his back. "So this is the plan, is it?"

"Seems as good a place to start as any."

The deputy nodded and reached for his hat, hanging on a peg on the wall. "If we're walking, having a tired old man in tow sure ain't gonna pose no threat then."

"You can hang back if you'd like…"

Wilfred laughed. "I ain't *that* old. Besides," he looked at Peter, "if the kid's keeping an eye on you, I better keep an eye on him. Teamwork and all."

Peter grinned at the idea. "So where are we headed?"

"Up north a ways. Top of the hill."

Peter raised an eyebrow. "You sure we don't want the horses?"

"Maybe not horses," Wilfred said. "But I'm packing grub and water. C'mon, kid. You can help."

***

It wasn't a long walk, but the rocky terrain, steep in some places and thick with brambles and brush, was difficult for feet and hooves alike. Johnny knew it was at least better to fall from a man's height than a horse's, and the slower pace would give him time to think.

It gave Peter, on the other hand, time to ask questions. And the boy had more than Johnny would've ever expected. Thankfully, Wilfred was more than willing to take on the task of answering.

"But if he's lying, and you know he's lying, but you can't *prove* he's lying, then what do you do?"

Peter was a bottomless pit of hypotheticals but, to his credit, was asking legitimate questions. More than once, Johnny had noticed the pause before Wilfred's answer, a clear indication that the boy was posing a situation that wasn't just a child's fantasy, but a realistic, well-thought-out scenario.

"Here's the thing," Wilfred said after a pause. "Think about town here. How many folks you see in a day?"

Peter shrugged. "A lot."

"Darn right," Wilfred said. "And out of that lot, some you know, some you recognize, some you never seen before, right?"

"Yeah."

"Well let's say you see somebody causing trouble one afternoon, maybe there's a row with Mac at the general store. You're gonna either know the fella, recognize him, or know you ain't never seen him before, right?"

"Right."

"And if you seen him again, you could probably say with a fair amount of certainty, 'yeah, Wilfred, that's the guy I seen.'"

"Right," Peter said again. Johnny heard a slight change in the boy's voice, as if this line of questioning was bringing up memories Peter hadn't intended.

"Well, I know you," Wilfred said, hurrying the talk along to keep Peter's mind occupied. "So if you tell me, 'that feller was giving Mac fits,' and that feller says 'no I warn't,' now we're getting somewhere."

"But what if there wasn't a witness?" Peter asked. "Or what if there's only one?"

"Everybody knows somebody," Wilfred said. "Just cause you don't see something happen don't mean you have no idea if it could." He paused for a moment to catch his breath. "For instance, you know me now. You just met me today, but let's say someone comes up to you and says he just seen me running down the street, jumping water troughs and eluding our fair sheriff here with my speed and agility. You gonna buy that story?"

Peter grinned. "Well, I suppose not."

"There ya go," Wilfred said. "Somebody's lying to you, you just start asking other folks. A fella might blow into town ain't none of seen before, but he had to blow in from somewhere, and folks sure musta seen him there."

Peter chewed on this for a moment. "But what if you don't know where he blew in from?"

Wilfred chuckled a little and started to respond when he suddenly cut himself off, his tired eyes becoming alert. Johnny had heard it too.

Off to their right, in the underbrush, a few stones trickled down the side of the hill. A branch shuddered as a body moved past it. Worse, there was the low, throaty growl.

Keeping his eye on the spot the sound was coming from, Johnny reached over, putting his hand on Peter's shoulder and moving the boy behind him. He didn't have to look to know Wilfred was doing the same, putting the boy at the center of a clock with Wilfred and Johnny looking at twelve and six.

"What is it?" Peter's voice was quiet, just above a whisper.

Johnny reached down and unholstered his revolvers. The rifle, his ideal weapon in this situation, was still locked away in the office. He hadn't planned on any excitement during the trip, and even with its strap, the gun had seemed an unnecessary burden. Now he wished he had the long-range accuracy it would've provided.

"Just stay calm," Johnny heard Wilfred whisper. "Keep yourself right where ya are and you'll be fine."

Ahead, about ten paces off, a coyote pushed through the underbrush. The daylight interaction was enough to make Johnny wary, but the animal's gaunt, visible ribs, the wild look in its eyes, and the drool dripping from its jowls told him this wouldn't be an animal he could just run off.

As if on cue, at what would be his ten and two o'clock, another pair of mangy animals stepped into view.

"I got three," he said to Wilfred, keeping his voice clear but soft.

"Nothing back this way," the deputy said. "How far you lookin'?"

"Ten paces." Johnny wasn't overly afraid of the animals. He'd dealt with worse situations, but never with a fifteen-year-old protege in tow. What the kid did could mean the difference between a quick show-down, or a bloody battle. "Peter," he said. "I need you to do one thing."

"O-k-k-kay."

The stutter. It could be good or bad. Johnny just had to hope that the kid's nerves would keep him frozen in place. "It's a real simple job," Johnny said, keeping his tone almost conversational. "All you gotta do is keep your eyes ahead of you. If you can see my back or Wilfred's you're right where you gotta be. This ain't gonna take but a second. You just stay behind one of us. You can handle that?"

"I th-th-thi ..." Johnny heard a frustrated sigh behind him, then, "Yes."

"Good." Johnny slowly moved his arms up into firing position, sighting in on the animals on the sides. Three in front wasn't normal, but these dogs didn't look to be thinking too clearly anymore as it was. "You still good back there, Wilfred?"

"Nothin' yet," the man said. "Ready when you are."

Johnny was startled by a touch on his hip, just above his gunbelt. He flicked his glance down, briefly, just enough to see Peter's hand, and above that, his face, looking around to see the threat. *Brave kid.*

"All right," Johnny said. "I'm going on three."

He watched the animals down the barrels of his guns. It was almost as if they were planning their attack as well. The two on the edges had their heads lowered, their forepaws inching slowly ahead.

"One." Johnny looked left and right, slowing her breath.

"Two."

That was when he saw it. The center coyote, though slightly farther away, hunkered down as well, though not with the anxious hunger of the others. This one bent back on its haunches. It made eye contact with Johnny, a string of drool trickling from its mouth.

The coyote lunged.

"Three!"

Johnny fired his guns simultaneously, immediately bringing the revolvers to the center in front of him, firing another pair of shots slightly above where the beast had been.

A short yelp was the only response.

He felt Peter's hand tight on his side. The wisps of smoke from the gun barrels drifted almost casually in the breeze. Ahead of him, the three mangy coyotes lay bleeding in the dirt. The two on the sides had hit the ground where they stood. The third, caught mid-jump – as he'd anticipated – had been flipped onto its back, one paw twitching slightly in the air.

"You still okay back there?" he said.

"Yeah." Both Wilfred and Peter answered at the same time, though the boy's reply was stretched out a bit by his still-present stutter.

Johnny smiled a little.

"Are they r-r-r … they mad?" Peter asked from under his arm.

The sheriff holstered the gun in his left hand and reached back, bringing the boy around to his side. "Could be," he said. "But you're the detective in training. What do you think most likely brought them on us?"

Peter shrugged, then, feeling the weight the motion brough to his shoulder, looked up at Johnny. He patted the satchel hanging from his side. "Our l-lunch."

"I reckon you hit the nail on the head there. Now hang back just a second with Wilfred here. Gotta make sure they ain't playing possum."

Peter laughed. "Coyotes playin' p-possum."

Johnny walked over to the first dead animal, keeping his gun trained on it as he approached, but calling back to the boy as he moved. "You know what these rascals like more'n anything?"

"W-what?"

"If you run." He moved from the first carcass to the second. "They get a kick out of chasin' you down. Like a game." Seeing the gaping hole in the animal's upturned chest, he moved to the third. "So when you stood your ground like ya did, that was the best thing you coulda done." He wasn't sure if it would work, but that stutter advertised the nerves Peter was still feeling. "So it seems to me, you done outsmarted your first pack of coyotes without even meaning to." He passed the third dog. The bullet had caught it in the head. No need for concern there anymore. He walked back toward Peter and Wilfred.

"The thing with being a lawman," Johnny continued, "is that you gotta be able to trust your gut. You gotta stay calm. If you'da run just now, we'd still be chasing after you. But you didn't. You turned around and faced your problem head on. That takes grit and a good brain. You done a fine job."

He holstered his gun, trying to be nonchalant while still assessing if his words had any impact on the boy's mind.

A quick glance at Peter's ear-to-ear grin was good enough.

"Nice work, kid," Wilfred said, patting Peter on the shoulder. "But since we're talking about lunch, what say we move up a bit and have us a bite? I ain't too keen on eating around what just tried to eat me."

Johnny was nervous the idea would put Peter to stuttering again, but the cool demeanor of the old deputy seemed to almost put the boy more at ease than anything Johnny had said so far.

"Sounds like a good plan to me," Peter said, falling in step as the two men continued up the trail. Johnny smiled when he heard the boy call back as they moved. "Not today, coyotes."

Chapter Twenty-Seven

It was early afternoon when the three finally reached the peak of the hill. The sun was burning in a clear blue sky and, had it not been for the strenuous nature of the climb, it could have made for a pleasant morning expedition. Wilfred breathed in a deep, slow rhythm and even Peter had lost some of the curiosity he'd shown at the beginning of the hike. The boy no longer darted from spot to spot, examining every overturned stone and peppering the lawmen with questions. Instead, he had reduced his inquiries to a simple, "We oughtta be pretty close by now, right?" tossed out occasionally to either of the two men.

Johnny stopped at the top of the incline. As the leader of the group, he waited for his two companions to join him in admiring the view, as well as take a perhaps more appreciated moment to regain their wind. Back behind them, the city could be seen in its miniscule sprawl across the dark earth.

"Don't look like so much from up here, does it?" Peter said, his hands on his hips, his chest expanding with breath.

"It's good for keeping what's important in mind," Johnny said. He pointed down toward the center of the town. "Right there, you can see where we started out. The sheriff's station is just about plum middle in the town."

"And there's the schoolhouse," Peter pointed, shading his eyes with one hand. "Which means your house is ..."

"Fellas," Wilfred's voice came clearly yet controlled from behind them. "We ain't alone up here."

"I was hoping not," Johnny started. The lightheartedness left his voice when he saw what Wilfred was referring to. A half dozen or so dogs were slowly working their way toward the group.

It was a motley pack, though not as mangy as, and certainly more well-fed than the coyotes below. But the gleam in the eyes of the animals was all too familiar.

Without a word, and without being told, Johnny felt Peter move behind him again. The sheriff let his hands fall to his revolvers, but for the moment, left them holstered.

"Today ain't our day," he heard Wilfred mutter.

A movement off to their right, at the edge of a small grove of trees, caught Johnny's eye. "We may not be in quite the spot we thought though," he said.

Just then, a piercing whistle cut through the air. The dogs, moving almost as one, halted in their approach, their collective ears perking up at the sound. A few even sat down on their haunches, as if the sound were a signal that all was well.

In fact, Johnny realized, watching the shape from the woods approach, that was precisely what it had been.

He reached back and moved Peter from behind him. "It's all right," he said. "Just a welcoming committee."

"Don't seem none too welcoming to me," the boy said, standing by Johnny and not moving too far away.

The sheriff pointed off to the right, where the shape was now clearly that of a man silhouette in the bright sunlight. "That's the fella we came to find, I reckon. Though it looks like he found us first."

"Howdy," the man called over, waving a hand in the air. "Don't mind them dogs. More bark'n bite." He walked leisurely toward them, a slight limp in his gait. He muttered a few words to the dogs and, all threat seemingly forgotten, the animals bounded off, some to the man, a few off to the woods. One tired looking hounddog simply flopped down on the earth where it sat, tongue lolling out to one side.

"What can I do for ya?" the man asked as he approached. "I was hoping you was the mail. Been runnin' a bit slow of late."

"Gonna have to disappoint ya there," Johnny replied. "Though I reckon a fella livin' up here is probably used to things takin' a little longer."

The man laughed. "You got that right." He reached out his hand as he crossed the last few paces. "Sheriff, eh?" He looked at Wilfred and then Peter. "Well, if this is your posse, I reckon it can't be nothin' too deadly serious. C'mon back to the house. Y'all could use a good sit after that hike I reckon."

Wilfred looked over at Johnny, who merely nodded, and the three followed the stranger back toward the edge of the woods.

***

The cabin sat just behind the treeline. It was a simple, two-room shack, built specifically for the convenience of the man and his dogs. A long, covered porch ran along one side, but it was the pair of rocking chairs that sat on it which really caught the trio's eyes.

"We'll drag these in," the man said, moving toward the door, a chair in each hand. "I reckon we can make something work for four."

Inside, the air was markedly cooler. Open windows let in a cool breeze and, within moments, the man had stepped out and returned with a bucket of cool water from a spring close by.

"If that don't wet your whistle," he pulled a crock off a small wooden table in the corner, "we can at least put a little pep in your step."

Johnny smiled. Peter, sitting on a stool and leaning back against the wall, leaned forward.

The man laughed. "Don't know if this'll be quite to your liking there, youngun, but you made the hike like the rest of us. Wouldn't be right to turn ya down. Name's Trevor McKenzie by the way. You'll have to pardon my manners. I talk to the doggies but they don't seem to have much to say in return." He poured out four small mugs from the crock, passing them around. "What brings y'all up this way?"

"You do," Johnny said, watching Peter as the boy sniffed the glass, then took a small, experimental sip.

Peter sputtered, the drink bursting back forth from his lips and dribbling down his chin.

"First time?" Trevor laughed.

Peter nodded, wiping his mouth with the back of his hand. "*That's* whiskey? I don't know how people can stand that."

Trevor laughed again. "Cause it ain't whiskey. That's moonshine, my boy. My own concoction." He poured a glass of water and handed it acoss. "That might be more to your liking."

Peter smiled weakly and downed the water, sloshing it in his mouth to try and get rid of the foul taste.

"Ya come lookin' for me, did ya?" Trevor continued, settling into a straight-backed chair. He had a gray beard, not too long, but certainly not maintained like a man who entertained visitors too often. His matching silver hair hung over his ears and, though the man was no doubt the oldest in the group, his days of living so far from town had certainly kept him in good form.

"We did," Johnny said. "Not on account of anything you done, mind ya. Just got some questions."

"Musta been on accounta something, though," Trevor said. "Heck of a hike for shootin' the breeze."

Johnny looked over at Wilfred. The deputy and the loner might have more in common, given the age difference between Johnny and Trevor, but Wilfred seemed content, as usual, to let Johnny run the show.

"You mentioned the mail earlier," Johnny said. "And it so happens that does have at least a little to do with why we come up here. You been writing with a fella by the name of Coy McDill?"

Trevor looked down into his mug of moonshine and thought for a moment. "Reckon you already know the answer to that or you wouldn't've come all this way. What's the fella got hisself into now?"

"Well, to be frank," Johnny said, "he got hisself into the cemetery. Found him shot out in the scrub not too long ago. Problem is, there aren't too many folks in town who can say they had the pleasure of knowing him."

Trevor smiled sadly. "I always kind of figured it'd come to this. I don't know if you mean what you say there, about the pleasure of knowing him. Coy had a way of making enemies in his younger days, but I can tell ya, hand to God, it was a pleasure knowing him the time that I did. Just wish he'd've listened to me more."

Johnny could see Peter out of the corner of his eye. This was the boy's first real interrogation and he wanted to make sure Peter was learning the right way to do it. Questioning wasn't all about shouts and accusations; folks were always more likely to speak if you treated them with respect, at least till they showed you to do otherwise.

"Father Brandon told us a real similar thing," Johnny continued. "Said Coy was about as model a citizen as he could hope for, at least when he saw him. But, as you can figure, we didn't walk up here to talk about the man's higher qualities, whatever they may've been."

"The gold, is it?"

Johnny was surprised. He'd assumed the man would be wily, if not outright deny it all, when it came to the gold. "As a matter of fact, it is. Sounds like you might be able to help us out some."

"I don't know how much help I'll be, but I'll do what I can."

Johnny made a 'go-ahead' gesture with his mug.

"Well, seeing as how Coy ain't with us no longer, I don't suppose talking's gonna do much harm now. Thing to remember is, these are just stories. I can't swear on none of it as being the honest truth, just what I heard and tried to piece together on my own."

"Same thing we're trying to do," Johnny said.

"Then I reckon you pieced together that was the Wells-Fargo gold."

Johnny nodded.

"Lots of stories about that there robbery. Half of 'em ain't true." The man laughed. "Most of 'em ain't true, I s'pose. Before you get any ideas, I wasn't there for it. I didn't meet Coy till much later. He was already pallin' around with the pastor by then. Met him through Brandon, in fact." Trevor looked down at his mug again, sorting out the past in his mind. "Ain't none of that too pressin' at the moment though. Facts as well as I know 'em is this: Coy pulled that Fargo job on his own, or at least, he's the last one left of the group that did it. They tucked that gold off somewhere for the time being, thinking they'd come back and get it when things settled down.

"But," he sighed. "You know how gold gets to a man. Double-crosses and suspicions and some say outright murder. Whatever it was, Coy was left with it and, to be real clear with ya, he was of a mind to hand it all over to the church. Problem is, them Kansas boys found out about it one way or another. After that, Coy didn't spend a second of his days not looking over his shoulder."

"So Dane Kansas had nothing to do with the robbery?" Wilfred interjected, surprised.

Trevor shrugged. "Not in any way I can figure. And Coy ... well, you may not believe this, but I'm of the mind that, if he coulda just passed the gold off to Kansas and been done with it, he woulda."

"But he could've," Johnny said.

Trevor laughed quietly. "He could've. You're right. But, Coy was a complicated fella. Way he saw it, he needed to make amends for what he done. Handing the gold over to somebody like Kansas was just perpetuatin' the problem." He looked at Peter and grinned. "There's a word for ya, kid." He sipped his moonshine and continued. "Coy got it in his head that the only way to make up for what he done was to work it off. He coulda gone to lock-up, but in his mind, he wouldn't be doing nothing there but sitting and eating free food. Figured if he could use the money for something good and really work at his sins, well, maybe he'd put some of those demons to rest."

"So he was protecting it," Johnny mused.

"I reckon that's about the best way to put it," Trevor said. "Ill-gotten gains, nonetheless, and the good book says your past comes back to haunt ya. Or at least something along those lines. Sounds like old Coy's past finally found him."

Johnny shook his head. "I don't know if I can see Dane Kansas as the avenging hand of the Lord in this."

Trevor shrugged. "Like I said, it's complicated. But you asked what I know, and that's the best I can give ya. Old Coy was determined to hand that money over. Sounds like he just didn't get his chance."

"Y'all wrote a lot of letters," Johnny said, trying to turn things back to facts. "I don't suppose there's anything in there I missed."

"You mean like where the gold's at?" Trevor sighed. "He never offered; I never asked. A secret like that, well, for an old man like myself, that's one I don't have any interest in knowing. The money's been bathed in blood since Coy got his hands on it and it sounds like it ain't done yet. Me, I'm all right here with my dogs."

"And your moonshine."

The man laughed. "A little vice comes with the territory."

Johnny looked across at Wilfred. The man seemed satisfied enough. Peter, for his part, was doing little to hide the look of disappointment on his face. But, Johnny thought, the man made a good point. Sometimes a good, quiet life was the best a man could hope for. He stood up, knocked back the remainder of his moonshine, and stuck out a hand.

"I reckon that's what we come to find out then," he shook with Trevor. "We may be crossin' paths again, but I appreciate your honesty and I assure you it won't be bringing you no trouble."

Trevor laughed. "Not knowing much ain't always a bad thing." He dropped a wink at Peter. "But don't tell your ma I told ya that. You keep at them books." He glanced at Johnny. "Or is he in training?"

Johnny laughed. "Just curious."

"All right, then," Trevor said. "Y'all're more'n welcome to stay and sit a spell. Walk back ain't no shorter than the one here."

"But the walk down is alway easier than the one up," Wilfred said, sitting his mug on the windowsill. "'Preciate the hospitality."

"Anytime," Trevor said, walking the trio to the door. "But next time, bring the mail if ya could."

Chapter Twenty-Eight

They were about halfway back to town when Johnny thought he heard something off to his left. They'd passed the coyotes about an hour previously, or at least what was left of them; the vultures and other scavengers hadn't wasted any time sniffing out the free meal. The problem here was that, as they came farther down the hill, the sparse thickets and weeds of higher up regained their foothold on the area. About a quarter hour previous, the trees had begun reaching up to their full height again and, while the three weren't in the woods proper, it made it nearly impossible to see what was, and all the easier for any lurking predators to see them.

"So you said since *he* knew Coy and we have to find people who know people, and *Coy* knew Kansas ..." Peter's review of the conversation had been non-stop ever since the boy knew they were out of earshot of the old man at the top of the hill, but now, even his voice trailed off.

The kid's ears were good. Whether that was due to the dangerous situations he'd found himself in lately, or if he was just finally starting to hone in on his surroundings, Johnny couldn't be sure. All he knew was that when one man might make a mistake, three almost assuredly would not.

He looked back at Wilfred, unsurprised to see the old man looking off in the same direction as Johnny himself.

"Not more dogs, is it?" Peter asked. Johnny was pleased to hear the boy's voice was still calm, but at a lower volume.

"Could be something passin' through," Wilfred said softly. "Deer. Fox. Coon."

Could be, Johnny thought, *but we both know it wasn't.*

The boy must have sensed the tension in the air. Johnny heard Peter move up the trail behind him and then, without direction, the boy hunkered down. The grasses here weren't the tall, thick cover found out farther in the prairies, but it would make the boy harder to see, something he seemed to instinctively know. Behind him, he heard Wilfred draw and cock his revolvers.

He looked back at Wilfred. The old man had stayed put, another sign that even Wilfred didn't believe the disturbance was just from a passing animal. The farther apart they stayed, the more difficult targets they made. Wilfred held his guns, barrel up, and nodded to Johnny.

"This is Sheriff John Steele, requesting you to come out and–"

It was as far as he got before the first gunshot exploded from the trees.

Johnny hit the dirt quickly, pushing Peter even lower, till the boy was flat on his stomach. *"Don't move unless I tell ya,"* he hissed as dirt kicked up around them. He tossed a quick glance back toward Wilfred, but the man was already belly-down in the grass, his guns held out ahead of him. It wasn't an ideal position, but he would have to make it work.

Johnny rose to a knee, keeping his shoulders hunched. He heard, almost felt, a bullet whiz by his ear. This was no time for the typical sheriff spiel. No amount of talking was going to stop whoever these men were.

The sheriff peered through the tall grass. Movement at the edge of the treeline was all he had to go on, but he knew it would be more than enough. Most of the time, showing a little grit was enough to send your enemy scurrying.

He fired twice, quickly, aiming – in a general sense – toward where he had to assume their assailants hid. It was luck more than skill, but a hollered curse let him know he hadn't been too far off his mark.

The firing made things more precarious for himself, and more importantly, the boy, though. Johnny reached a hand down and touched Peter's back. *"Stay right here."*

On hands and knees, Johnny crawled a few paces away, hoping to keep the stray bullets away from the young man. To his left, he heard Wilfred fire a few times in fast succession. Johnny poked his head up, just in time to see a rider emerge from the edge of the woods. A rifle gleamed in the man's hands, but a bandana obscured his face. Without doubt, Johnny could see the barrel was pointed directly towards Wilfred's place in the grass.

The sheriff came up to a kneeling position, aware of the risk, but not taking time to consider it. He fired quickly. The man was crosswise to him, so the target his side provided was small, but it was enough. Johnny's second shot caught the man in the arm, spinning him slightly in the saddle. His rifle roared, but without a steadying hand, the bullet shot harmlessly off in the air.

The horse reared up and the rider, grasping at the pommel with his one good hand, managed to turn the animal back toward the woods. Emboldened, Johnny fired into the underbrush, both guns spitting fire from the barrels as the deafening roar from the pieces filled the air.

A whinny. The rattle of hooves. A few half-heard yells and broken words came from behind the tree cover, then the rhythmic sounds of horses in retreat.

Johnny held his position a moment longer, eyeing the dim treeline as best he could. As the sounds faded, he hollered over to Wilfred.

"Everything all right over there?"

"Wish it had been a bear," the old man called back.

"Peter?"

The silence, though it lasted only a split second, made Johnny's stomach drop. Even then, the uncertainty in the boy's voice did little to raise his spirits.

"Y-y-yeah," he heard, followed by a rustling in the grass as the boy moved. "I think I'm okay. I ... I don't know."

Johnny rushed over. After a shoot-out, you needed to know. There was no room for uncertainty.

Peter was up and Johnny had his hands on his shoulders in an instant. The youth winced, but didn't cry out. Johnny held him at arm's length, finally seeing the slowly darkening spot on the boy's upper sleeve. Johnny hooked his fingers in the hole in the material, ripping the sleeve free and jerking it down the boy's arm.

"Am I sh-sh-shot?"

Johnny loosed his canteen from around his shoulders and poured water over Peter's arm. The boy winced, gritting his teeth. As the blood washed away, Johnny could see a red crease in Peter's upper arm. But no hole. Thank goodness, no hole.

Johnny sat back on his heels, a sigh of relief escaping him. He looked up at Peter. The boy's eyes were wide, his face white.

"Not shot," Johnny said, reaching down for the discarded sleeve. "Winged."

Wilfred, having made his way over to the group, leaned down to examine the wound. "Gonna take more than that to put you down." He patted the boy on the opposite shoulder.

"They winged me," Peter said, almost to himself.

Johnny poured water over the fabric and reached up to put it around the boy's arm, using the torn sleeve as a makeshift bandage. He worked smoothly, methodically, but all the while, he couldn't help but notice how, now that the situation was assessed, the boy's stutter was gone.

"Happens to the best of us," Wilfred said. "Got one just like it myself."

"Really?" Peter twisted back to see the deputy.

"Really," Wilfred said. "Same spot, even."

Johnny smiled to himself. Surely part of it was just shock and the boy would be feeling a little less chipper come evening, but Wilfred was certainly downplaying the situation and it seemed to help.

The sheriff tightened the sleeve over Peter's arm and stood up to look at the young man. "Well, I'll tell ya, all things considered, getting winged ain't a bad ending to the day. That's, what?" he looked at Wilfred. "Three coyotes, six dogs, a hermit, and a gunfight? I don't know about this one. Seems like me and you haven't had this much adventure in a good long while."

Peter grinned up at the man. "Maybe next time I can have a gun."

"You know," Johnny said, turning and starting down the trail again. "That idea ain't half bad. For now, let's get ya home before anything else tries to put an end to us early."

Chapter Twenty-Nine

Etta looked over at the sky. The sun seemed to move slower when Peter was away, especially when she didn't know where he was. Sheriff or no sheriff, she didn't like having her boy out wandering the town. Things had been bad enough when he'd roughhouse with the other boys at school. Now, though ...

She shook her head. Even thinking about the men looking for her Peter made her sick. Perhaps with Johnny was indeed the safest place Peter could be, but it didn't change the fact she wished they could just disappear. Just pack up, hop on a train, and be done with the town.

Then again, as she well knew, just because they moved on didn't mean Dane Kansas would. And, as she also knew, moving into a new town would do nothing to ease the same old questions: *Where's his daddy? Who was his daddy? Don't you think you oughtta be looking for a husband?*

Some things she was cursed to endure no matter what.

She reached down into the basket at her feet, pulling out one of Johnny's shirts and pinning it to the line hanging across the side yard. She would do anything she could to help this be over, but the truth was, she didn't see any way it could be over. Maybe different for a time, but as long as she and Peter were alive, the truth of their past would haunt her.

Voices caught her attention, and the clip clop of hooves coming down the path to the house. She shielded her eyes against the sun and could just make out the two figures she'd been longing to see. Unfortunately, the early return did little to ease the tension in her stomach. Why would they be back so soon? What could've happened?

Trying to control her nerves, Etta tossed the few clothespins in her hand into the basket at her feet and walked over to meet the pair at the front of the house. She couldn't be sure, but something seemed different. The way Peter sat in the saddle wasn't as an awkward youth. He moved with the animal. There was a confidence in the way he held himself. She should've been proud, she knew, but it was like her boy had left and a man had returned. She hurried the last few paces, her eyes widening as the pair dismounted.

"Now, listen ..." Johnny tried to start.

"Peter! Your shirt! Your arm!" Etta ran over to the boy, kneeling down in front of him and taking the injured limb in her hands.

Peter jerked back. "Ain't nothing to be concerned over. I'm all right." He took a step back and looked over at Johnny. "Just part of the job."

Etta looked at her boy, dumbstruck. The two had had their fair share of rows, but never had she been so off-handedly dismissed by him before. She stood up, her mouth open, words starting and stopping as she looked down at her dusty, injured son.

Johnny stepped forward before she could speak.

"We're gonna need us just a minute, I believe," he said, leading Peter into the house.

Etta couldn't hear exactly what the man said; his voice was low, almost inaudible, but by the tone, she could be quite sure Johnny had had no trouble finding the words that had eluded her.

***

Inside, Johnny turned a chair out with the toe of his boot and pointed at it. He moved over to a small cupboard, rooting around inside until he found a roll of cotton bandaging. He heard the familiar creak of the wooden seat as Peter sat down.

"That will be the last time I hear that tone come out of you," Johnny said, standing up and walking over to the boy. Peter's head hung low, a sure sign that he knew he'd earned his reprimand. "I ain't looking to spend my days with someone who ain't got no respect for their own ma. You understand?"

Peter nodded silently.

Using his pocket knife, Johnny cut a few lengths of material and sat the remainder of the roll on the counter. He wetted the first piece from a pitcher of water on the table. Dampening the sleeve around Peter's arm, he changed tactics slightly.

"You know why I'm getting this wet first?"

Peter shrugged.

"C'mon. You made a mistake. You'll apologize for it. But we ain't gonna cry over it all night. You're wanting to act a grown up, that's part of being one. You be responsible for what you done and you know it don't let you off the hook none. You're still learning today. Now why am I getting this wet?"

Peter was silent a few moments longer, almost to the point Johnny felt the boy wouldn't speak the rest of the night. "So it don't stick."

"That's right," Johnny said. "If I was to pull that ratty sleeve off there, you'd just start bleeding all over again." He squeezed water from the cotton, soaking the sleeve as best he could. "You figure that out on your own?"

"Nah," Peter said. "Ma. She ..."

Before he could continue, Etta came through the door. Her eyes were dry, but the look in them told Johnny her emotions were still in turmoil.

"Had a bit of a tumble out in the prairie grass there," Johnny said, looking up to make eye contact with Peter. "It was a long day."

"I see." Etta stood at the kitchen counter behind them.

"That's probably why our tempers are running a little high, ain't it?" he looked at Peter.

"Yes, sir."

"Anything else?" Johnny looked at the youth.

"I apologize for the way I spoke to you just now, Ma. It was rude and inconsiderate. It won't happen again."

"Well, I ..." Johnny could see the woman wringing her hands off to his side. "I appreciate that. I didn't mean to ..."

Johnny stood up. "You don't have nothing to apologize for. Tell ya what. We had a long dusty day. You been here on your own. How about I take care of this here scrape, you get us some dinner going, and we can all just sit down and have a chat?"

Etta looked at him almost as if she didn't believe it could be that easy. But, after a moment, she turned back toward the cupboards. "I did go into the general store this morning ..."

"Excellent," Johnny said. "I'm starved."

***

Regardless of the tension on their return, Etta was able to cook up a wonderful, warm, and filling meal. Peter, for his part, having gotten over the chagrin of being reprimanded by the man he held in such high esteem, quickly found himself rattling off tales of their adventure, though, Johnny was relieved to see, the mundane aspects were rather exaggerated, while the more adventurous parts were somehow skimmed over.

"It was a real interrogation, ma," Peter was saying. His plate was empty, but his fork moved through the air, punctuating the telling of his story. "But not like you think. See, you don't just get in there and holler. You gotta be smooth. You gotta get 'em to like you. Then they open right up. Shoot, he even gave us some of his ..." he looked down for a minute. "He went out to the spring there and got water just for us. And we sat in his house and everything. I never even knowed anybody lived out that way."

Etta eyed Johnny throughout the telling, and the sheriff did his best to insert reassurances where he felt it appropriate.

"More like gathering information," Johnny said. "The man wasn't suspected of nothing but writing some letters. But your boy's right. Treat folks decent and they're a lot more helpful."

"And Wilfred," Peter continued. "I know Johnny knows just about everything there is to know. But Wilfred, on accounta being old, I guess, well he knows darn near everything!" He spread his arms wide, enhancing the word with a gesture. Unfortunately, he caught the edge of his plate with this elbow, sending the piece to shatter on the hardwood floor.

"Peter!"

"It's all right, it's all right," Johnny stood up. "Can't fault a fella for being excited. I'll get it. Can't have him scraping himself up any more'n he already has."

Johnny saw Etta's gaze at Peter and wondered if there was another talking-to in the young man's immediate future. "Why don't you go get yourself cleaned up?" he said to the boy. "Wash some of that trail dust off your neck."

Seeing his chance at least a momentary reprieve, Peter dashed outside toward the hand-pump.

"Don't you think he's getting away with this," Etta said, kneeling down beside Johnny as the sheriff picked up a few shards of the plate's remains.

Johnny laughed. "Oh I know he ain't. But I figured he don't need me standing there when you give it to him."

Etta paused. "Johnny, whatever happened out there today … are we safe?"

Kneeling there on the floor together, Johnny held her gaze. Without thinking, he reached over and took her hand. "As long as I'm around, I promise you there ain't nothing I won't do to keep you two safe."

Etta looked down at her hand, drawing Johnny's gaze. His hand, dark, lined, and calloused, only brought out the femininity in her own delicate features. He felt his stomach jump as she looked back up at him, their eyes meeting.

Peter burst back in through the door. "Can't get the pump pumping," he said, breaking the moment.

"I'll be right there," Johnny said. He hesitantly removed his hand from Etta's, though, he thought at least, there seemed to be some reluctance on her part as well.

Chapter Thirty

Later that evening, as the sun was still making its leisurely way toward the horizon, Johnny knocked on Peter's door and gestured for the boy to follow him outside.

In the backyard, Johnny had set up three pieces of firewood at various distances and he led the boy to a stick lying in the grass.

"From here," he pointed to the stick, "you got ten, fifteen, and twenty paces to them logs. I ain't expecting you to be no master here, but I want you to get used to judging things by how far away they look. That's gonna be important in a lotta ways, but for the time being, you just get used to the way things look. Ain't always that everything's gonna be standing nice and still like this."

Peter looked at the sheriff and shrugged. He stood at the stick, his hands in his pockets, eyeing the placement of the logs.

"The farther away something is, the less likely you are to get a good bead on it," Johnny was saying. If it's running, you gotta figure which way it's gonna go. It may drop straight down. It may cut back. It may turn and come straight for ya."

"Like the coyotes," Peter said.

"Exactly like the coyotes."

"Or like," Peter looked back over his shoulder at the house. "Well, you know."

"That's right," Johnny said. "For as long as we're doing this though, I want you thinking about them coyotes. That's the only way I talked your ma into this after all."

Johnny reached down and unholstered one of his revolvers, holding it out in the palm of his hand so the boy could see it without grabbing on immediately. "I'm sure you've heard a lot about these, but I want you to put all that aside for right now. This here's a lump of metal. It ain't good or bad or anywhere in between. It ain't a whole lot different than the fork you had in there at supper. You can use it for good or you can use it for bad, but the thing itself, it's just a tool."

He opened the loading gate and turned the cylinder, showing the boy the butt end of the bullets. "This here is where the bullets go in," he pointed to the end of the barrel with a slight smile, "and this here is where they come out."

Peter rolled his eyes.

"You know what single-action means?" Johnny asked.

"It just does one thing," Peter said. "Kills stuff."

Johnny started to respond, then caught himself. "Y'know," he said. "That ain't a bad way for you to think of it right now. But what I mean is here," he pointed to the trigger. "This trigger only does one thing. It has a single action. The trigger makes this," he pointed to the hammer, "fall. The hammer hits the bullet, the bullet comes out the barrel. As long as this hammer ain't back, you aren't gonna do nothing but wear out your finger."

He flipped the gun around and held it by the barrel, offering the butt to the boy. "Keep it pointed down anyway. But grab on here. I want you to feel the weight."

To Johnny's relief, Peter took the gun carefully, making sure to keep his finger outside the guard, but still holding the gun in a nearly proper way.

"It's heavy," Peter said, looking down at the weapon.

"That's how you know it ain't a toy. A horse is heavy. A wagon is heavy. These here weapons are heavy too. Not something you wanna be playing around with. Now," he turned Peter so the boy was facing the logs. "Bring this up like so, both hands," he reached over, adjusting the boy's grip on the gun. "You're gonna look down here," he ran his finger along the barrel. "Line up your sights and what it is you're wanting to hit."

Johnny adjusted Peter's hands and shoulders slightly. "Both eyes open," he said. "That one eye nonsense ain't gonna do you no good unless you only ever shoot at logs. Focus on the wood there." He paused, letting the boy steady himself and get familiar with the foreign activity. "Now, reach up with your thumb, and cock the hammer back. Check your aim again ... breathe slow ..." He could feel the tenseness in Peter's arms. It was a good sign. The ease and nonchalance would come soon enough. For now, he wanted the boy to stay focused on the importance of what he was learning.

"The gun's gonna kick, but that's all right. Keep your feet steady, lean forward just a bit." He reached up and adjusted the boy's hands. "Let it kick. Up." He moved the gun, mimicking the motion. "When you're ready, squeeze."

A few seconds later the gun roared in Peter's hands, its barrel kicking up, and dirt exploded in the yard in front of the log.

Peter looked over at him, eyes wide. "You do that with one hand?"

Johnny laughed. It wasn't the response he'd expected. "I got a few pounds on ya. But listen, this is the most important thing to pay attention to when you're holding a gun: where'd the bullet go?"

"In front of the log," Peter said, sounding disappointed. "Hit the dirt."

"Don't worry about missing," Johnny said. "What does it tell us about why you missed, though?"

"I ..." Peter looked down the barrel, moving it slightly up and down. "I was aiming too low?"

"Exactly. Now an easy one. How many shots left?"

"Five?"

Johnny nodded. "Let's see what you can do."

***

With the sun finally sinking behind the horizon, Johnny had Peter fire off the remaining bullets in the cylinder and then held out his hand for the gun. "Nighttime shooting is a whole different animal," he said. "Besides, aren't your ears ringing?"

"What?" Peter laughed, cupping a hand to the side of his head.

"C'mon," Johnny smiled. "Let's toss these logs back on the pile and head in. Your ma's probably had her fill of listening to us for one night."

"You'd think she'd be happy," Johnny heard Peter say softly as they walked out to pick up the now chipped and chinked logs.

"Why's that?"

Peter shrugged. "You're teaching me how to take care of myself. She's always so worried about me. Maybe now she can see I'm not a little kid she needs to protect."

Johnny smiled. "I'm afraid that's something that's never gonna change. You're her son, her only child, in fact. That woman is gonna worry about you with every breath she's got in her."

"Probably follow me around as a ghost or something, too."

"Could be worse," Johnny grabbed the third log and handed it to Peter. "Lotta folks got parents who couldn't care less about 'em. Some don't even know who their folks are. You need a moment to think about that, I'm happy to take you down by the orphanage. Them kids have some stories might make you think otherwise."

Peter hefted the log up onto his shoulder. "For all I know I am one of 'em."

Johnny stopped. "How ya figure that?"

Peter shrugged. "Well, half like 'em anyway. I don't know who my pa is."

"What's your ma say?"

Peter sighed. "About the same as Trevor told us earlier today. Stories. Never can know which one is true and which one ain't. Reckon it don't matter much anyway. Once folks figure you for a bastard, there ain't much you can do to convince 'em otherwise."

"That what you're always getting in rows about at school?"

"I s'pose," Peter looked down at the ground. "That. What they say about ma. All comes down to the same thing, I reckon. If I had a pa around, none of this would even be happening."

"C'mon," Johnny started toward the woodpile. "If you want my two cents, here's how I figure it. You got a mother in there doing everything she can to take care of you. Maybe it seems

171

like too much on some days. Maybe it don't seem like enough on others."

"I'm not sayin' that," Peter broke in quickly. "It's always more than enough."

"Then I'll say it for ya. Ain't no shame in wanting to grow up. But I'll ask this," he tossed the two logs on the pile and took Peter's, adding it to the top of the stack. "What do you know about my folks?"

Peter shrugged. "Nothin' I guess."

"That's cause they ain't been around for a long time. Having a family ain't always easy, but not havin' one ... well that's something I wouldn't wish on nobody."

"They died?"

Johnny felt his jaw tighten. It wasn't something he talked about with anyone, but something about the boy made him want to open up, even if it hurt. "They did. It's been a good long while now. But let me ask you this, what do you see when you see me? A fella with no family?"

"I see the sheriff, a'course," Peter said.

"What about Wilfred?"

"The deputy." Peter paused. "His family's all gone too?"

"Believe it or not, he's got a sister next town over," Johnny said. "The point is, after a while, it don't matter who you got and who you don't, it matters who *you* are. Them folks in your family, you do your best to make 'em proud whether they're still around or not. So maybe you don't know who your pa was." He put a hand on Peter's shoulder and started leading him back toward the house. "You do know who your ma is. You know what kind of man she hopes you'll be. And even if you didn't have her, you know in your heart what kind of man you want to be. You stick to that and can't nobody fault you for it."

Peter walked on in silence for a while. "Thing is, I don't think she wants me to be a man. Not yet anyway."

Johnny laughed. "Ain't nothing wrong with that. Mas are tricky. But there's one thing you don't need to lose sleep over. When she's worrying, when she's asking questions, when you feel like she won't let you stretch your legs and have your adventures, it's all on account of she loves you something fierce. Seems to me there's worse things in the world than that."

Chapter Thirty-One

The next morning, Johnny and Wilfred sat in the sheriff's office. Coy's letters and diary were out on the desk in front of them and both men were leaning on the wood, foreheads in hands.

"I just don't see it," Wilfred said after a long pause. "I think Trevor was shooting straight. What's a guy like him gonna do at his age?"

Johnny looked at him, a wry grin on his face.

"Yeah, yeah," Wilfred said. "That's why you oughtta be listening to me. At *my* age, I don't got any interest in galavanting around digging for gold that may or may not be there. Especially not if it's gonna bring the likes of Dane Kansas down on me. That fella's got a good spread up there. A bit of a hike, but like he said, he's got his dogs and his 'shine. Ain't no sense in sitting on that gold."

Johnny leaned back in his chair and sighed. "I know it. You're right. I just can't help but think that gold's gotta be out there somewhere."

Just then, the front door to the office opened and the tall figure of Phil Anderson stepped in out of the morning light.

"How do, fellas?" Anderson said, taking his hat off and stepping across the room. "Any news on this end?"

Johnny laced his hands behind his head and stretched his legs out. "They say no news is good news, but I'm starting to think that ain't the case in this particular situation. You got any leads?"

Anderson pulled a chair over and sat down beside Wilfred. The older man scooted over slightly. "Nothing solid," he said.

"Most of what I'd call hunches. I was hoping to run some by ya."

"Shoot," Johnny said.

"Well the way I see it is this," Anderson leaned his elbows on his knees. "We got Coy, Kansas, and the gold all turning up in this area. Could be that Kansas just tracked Coy here, same as we did. Could be that the gold ain't nowhere near here, or it could be that there ain't no gold at all. But the thing I keep coming back to is this one fact. Coy's dead."

"Nothing gets past you Pinkerton boys," Wilfred laughed.

"All right, all right," Anderson said. "But let me finish. Let's say you're Coy, I'm Kansas. I find you on account of I'm sure you've got the gold. I pull a gun, tell ya you can either tell me or I shoot. What do you do?"

Johnny shrugged. "If those are the options, it sounds like Kansas shot, so Coy must not've given it up."

"That's the same conclusion I come to. And as backward as it seems, Kansas seems like just the kind of fella to shoot the only hope he had just outta spite. Temper on that man is legendary. And so's the pride. I figure, he's sure he's gonna find the gold one way or another and if Coy wasn't gonna make it easy on him, well, so be it."

"So what're you getting at then?" Johnny asked. "Kansas set out prospecting?"

"Nah," Anderson leaned back in his chair. "He's hot-headed, but he ain't stupid. I'm thinking Coy must've told him something. Even if it wasn't enough to save his life, it was enough to lead Kansas to believe that the gold could be found. My hunch is telling me there's a map somewhere."

Johnny folded his hands in his lap. "Sounds like our hunches are lining up pretty good then. So far anyway. Your hunch go beyond just the idea?"

"I figure we got two options. Either Coy kept it in his head, or he wrote it down. If Kansas had any inkling the man had it memorized, I imagine he'd think twice before putting a bullet in him. We just gotta figure out where Coy wrote it down."

Johnny gestured at the table in front of him. "You're welcome to point it out to us."

"This is all Coy's?"

"Everything we could get," Johnny said. He leaned forward and shifted the papers around. "Letters. A diary. Old bible. Wilfred and I been going through it bit by bit, but we ain't seen nothing here that jumps out at us."

"Interesting." Anderson leaned forward, his eyes hungrily taking in the papers. "If you want, I could take a look at them as well. Two heads are better than one, so three can't hurt, right?"

Johnny laughed a little. Something in the man's eagerness went beyond simply wanting to close a case. If he didn't know better, it was that same gold-hungry look he'd seen in so many men on their way out west. Like their better judgment was already teetering at the prospect of wealth. He glanced at Wilfred who, despite seeming uninterested, was keeping a wary eye on Anderson as well.

"I reckon I don't see what it can hurt. Here ya go," Johnny started gathering up a loose pile of papers from the desk. "Our best guess at the moment is that the clues, if there even are any, are in here."

Anderson eagerly grabbed at the papers, his eyes poring over them immediately. "Excellent, excellent," the man said.

"They're so commonplace. It would definitely be the best place to hide something." He looked quickly up at Johnny. "Would you mind terribly if I took these back to my room? I need to spread them out, I think. Get a feel for the man."

Johnny waved a hand. "Be my guest. Just keep us posted on what ya find. No sense in running out after Kansas all by your lonesome."

Anderson was already up and halfway to the door. "Of course. Pinkerton doesn't employ fools. You'll be the first to hear when I find something."

In a rush, Anderson was through the door and Johnny could hear the rapidly retreating boot steps on the wooden walkway.

Wilfred looked over at him. "You sure about that?"

Johnny shrugged. "If that man finds a map in the stack of chores Father Brandon gave out, I reckon he deserves to find the gold, too."

Wilfred laughed. "That's all you give him?"

Johnny smiled. "I don't see any sense in sending trouble up Tervor's way. And I had to give him something. That's about the only thing we got I'm sure the map *ain't* in."

The old deputy grinned. "I ain't sure the map's in any of it."

"We agree there, friend. But if it is, I aim to make sure one of us is the one to find it first."

***

Late that afternoon, after having sent Wilfred home for the day and nearly ready to go himself, Johnny leafed through the Bible on the desk in front of him. Underlined passages and margin notes in Coy's surprisingly fine hand jumped out at him, but none seemed to carry anything other than religious meaning. The letters to and from Trevor had been gone over so often Johnny almost felt like he could recite them.

He reached out and took up the journal once more. It seemed the most likely place for the man to leave himself clues. But again, other than the penmanship, the book appeared unremarkable.

Johnny flipped through the pages, continuing even through the blank ones at the back, the ones that would never be filled now. How could a man with such a secret leave no trace of it anywhere?

He sat the open book down on its face, the spine up, and leaned back in his chair, looking at the mess on his desk.

Then, it caught his eye.

Not believing his luck at first, Johnny leaned forward, getting his eyes level with the desktop. And there, plain as day, he could see it.

He reached in his pocket and pulled out his folding knife, opening the blade and carefully working the tip between the final page and the book's backing. It was just a small gap, but it was enough. Slowly, gingerly, he worked the blade around the edge of the book, breaking the glue that held the paper to the board.

In a moment's time, the book lay open, its inner cover exposed. And there, folded in quarters, was a dirty, well-worn piece of paper.

Johnny pushed the diary aside and unfolded the sheet on his desk. "You clever son of a gun," he whispered.

He reached into a desk drawer for a pencil and paper and, setting the map to one side, began to draw.

Chapter Thirty-Two

Etta sat on the edge of the deep tub, her fingers gliding back and forth in the steaming water. It had been a long day. A productive one, to be sure, but long nonetheless. And it wasn't that she was upset by the amount of work she found to do. The poor sheriff was much more in need of a woman than he even seemed to realize. But the additional mouth to feed, the extra clothes to clean, and the constant stress of their entire situation were taking their toll.

For once, if only for fifteen minutes, she was going to take some time for herself. Surely she'd earned that!

She stood up, loosening the cloth belt that cinched her plain brown dress just along her ribs. It was hardly the most fetching outfit she'd ever worn, but, she thought as she undid a few buttons below her throat, fetching wasn't exactly the same as functional.

She leaned down, lifting her skirts enough to unlace the strings of one tall boot, then the other. She sat back on the edge of the tub, pulling the tight-fitting shoes off and setting them aside. Even just getting out of those shoes for a few minutes was glorious. She felt like she'd been on her feet for a week. And despite what the traveling salesmen would have her believe, no calf-high boot was made for comfort in the hot summer days.

She kneaded the soles of her feet. There was still dinner to prepare. Still Peter to wrangle. That boy ... she sighed. At least she had Johnny on her side now. Even if the sheriff's star was the last thing she wanted for her son, at least she had a man to make her point alongside her. She could be the president of the United States and that boy wouldn't listen. Not at fifteen, at least.

She stood up and pulled her dress over her head, folding it carefully and putting it on top of her boots. Even with just one layer removed, she felt herself relaxing even more. Thank goodness she wasn't fighting a corset every day.

Etta unrolled her socks and removed her chemise, then stepped out of her pantalettes, laying the gauzy white garments on the pile with the rest. Even over the steam of the hot water, removing layer after layer of stifling clothing felt almost luxurious. She reached up and loosed her hair, tossing the thin rawhide thong onto the pile with the rest, and slowly slid her foot into the water.

She'd purposefully heated it to almost boiling it over the fire. Between the trips to fill the large tub, the temperature cooled enough on its own to make the water almost the perfect temperature. She leaned against the wall with one hand and eased her other foot in, enjoying the way the warmth slowly eased her aching muscles.

She heard the front door open and close again. Peter back from wherever he had run off to, she assumed. No doubt making a beeline to his room and his sheriffing books. All the years she'd spent trying to get him to read. Who would've thought this would be the thing to get him motivated?

The door to the small room burst open.

Etta screamed, her arms instinctively covering her body as she plopped low into the water. "Peter! How many times have I told you ..."

Her voice died on her lips as the blood rushed to her cheeks.

"I ... I ..."

"Go!" she yelled.

More than chagrined, and stuttering like her son, she watched the embarrassed sheriff stumble out of the room, pulling the door closed behind him.

Etta sunk lower in the water, her hands over her face.

It was his house, after all. But what was she to do? Never bathe? Put a sign on the door?

She let out a small groan, trying to hide herself in the clear, warm water and wash away the embarrassment of what had just happened.

***

Fully dressed again, Etta lingered in the bathroom. There were plenty of ways to have the conversation she was afraid she was about to have, but she could think through none of them without feeling her cheeks flush. If there were a way to avoid it altogether, slink out of the house and never come back, she'd be more than a little tempted to jump at the chance.

She patted her hair, felt at her collar. She was as proper as she was likely to get. And, a part of her thought, still a little irritated. Not just with Johnny; it was an honest mistake, she supposed, but at the whole situation. Why couldn't things just work out once in a while? All she'd wanted was a bath. To be alone. Just a few moments of peace.

Etta took a deep breath. Things weren't going to change just because she hoped they would, though. If life had taught her anything, it was that.

She straightened her back and walked out to the main room.

At the kitchen table sat Johnny, a paper on the table in front of him, his head in his hand, but his feigned nonchalance did nothing to hide his embarrassment. Etta watched him for a second and, to her surprise, felt herself relaxing somehow.

She cleared her throat. "Johnny."

"Ma'am," he turned to her. "I can't begin to tell you how sorry I am for what I done just now. It was rude and thoughtless and I feel awful about it."

"It was a surprise, to be sure," she said, walking over to the table. "But I ought to remember I'm in someone else's house."

"It don't matter whose house you're in," Johnny said, his eyes jumping around the room, "it's not proper to barge in on folks."

Etta looked at him. He was so different from other men she'd known. He was layered, complex. Most men would've hung in the door for a moment longer, enjoyed the surprise. Or perhaps blamed her for not using her head, for not thinking things through. Here she was, a guest in his home, and he was apologizing to her. And for what? Accidentally entering a room without knocking.

"Johnny," she folded her hands on the table. "We're both adults here. I understand that mistakes happen. What if we just put it behind us?"

His eyes lit on her for a moment and she saw the faintest smile at the corner of his lips. "If you want to do the forgivin', I'll do my best to forget …" he looked almost as if there was something else he wanted to say. His bashful smile gave it away.

She sighed. "Men are just big boys sometimes."

He laughed a little, the tension easing in the room. "I do apologize. It was thoughtless of me."

"Apology accepted," she said, forcing him to hold eye contact with her. "If it happens again, though, I'm afraid I'm going to have a few more questions for you."

Johnny smiled, his eyes catching the light of the dying sun and bringing butterflies to her stomach. "I'll do my best to see that it don't."

"All right," she said, somehow, surprisingly, feeling closer to the man than she had before. "So what is it that brought you home in such a huff?"

"This," he said, sliding the paper across the table to her.

Etta looked down, her eyes running across the lines and shapes on the paper. "Is this ...?"

"If it ain't, it sure fooled me."

"What're you going to do?"

Johnny leaned back in his chair and grinned. "Oh I got all kinds of plans for that."

Chapter Thirty-Three

That evening, Johnny, Wilfred, and Phil sat at the kitchen table. Etta had excused herself from the meeting, claiming that the less she knew about the lawmen's work, the less she had to worry about. This same theory did nothing to keep Peter away, however, and after nearly a quarter hour of begging, cajoling, and pleading, the youth secured himself a spot at the corner of the table as well.

"No wonder I couldn't find anything in the papers you gave me!" Phil exclaimed after Johnny had described his discovery in the book. "I was looking in the wrong place all along." He fell back in his chair with a sigh, running his hand through his hair. "As long as someone knows where to look, at least."

"That map'll only get us to the gold," Wilfred said, his voice an odd mix of both tired and curious. "It don't get you much closer to your goal."

"Well, perhaps, maybe not," Phil quickly tried to regain his standing. "But if we have what Dane wants, surely that's some leverage. Is it not?"

"Maybe," Johnny said. "To be honest, I ain't real sure what I want to do with it just yet."

"Where is it?" Phil asked eagerly. "We could go over it now and certainly, between the three of us, we can come up with a plan."

"Four," Peter said.

Phil gave the boy a brief look and then turned his eyes back to the sheriff. "Of course, four. Why not? But, the map?"

"I hope this don't come off as disrespectful to nobody," Johnny said slowly, "but we're talking about a lot of gold here. I didn't figure it was too wise for any of us to be gallivanting around town with a map like that in our pocket."

Phil sighed. "How are we to make a plan if we don't know where to execute it?"

"We'll get to that," Johnny said. "As for now, I figured it was safest if I just left the map where I found it so we can focus on the problem at hand."

"You left it in the office?" Phil perked up.

Johnny shrugged. "It's been safe enough tucked in the back of that book this long. Besides, who'd be foolish enough to break *into* the sheriff's office? Can't hardly drag folks down that way most the time."

Wilfred let his gaze rest on Johnny for a moment and then took a drink of the slowly-cooling coffee in his mug.

"Yes, yes," Phil said finally. "That does seem to hold water. I gotta say, I'm a little hemmed in by this, but I'm sure we can make something work. So what *is* your plan, exactly?"

"Well," Johnny took a deep breath. "I figure the first thing we gotta do is see if the map's even any good. I can't think of any reason why it wouldn't be. Coy went to all the trouble of hiding it and not telling nobody, and he didn't ever strike me as the most clever of fellas, rest his soul. So I figured, if it works for you all, we meet up tomorrow 'round noon and take ourselves a little wander to see where the map leads us. After that we can get the money somewhere safe. Then we can work on Kansas. I just ain't comfortable with the idea of that much gold simply laying about any longer than it's gotta."

Phil nodded slowly, the gears in his mind clearly turning. "Yes. Yes, that does seem to be the most logical course of action." He sat for a moment longer and then abruptly stood. "Well, if we're going to begin making moves on Kansas, I need to make sure Pinkerton is abreast of it. You know how bosses can be. Always wanting to know every little detail." He adjusted his hat on his head and turned to the door. "A pleasant evening gentlemen. I'll see you tomorrow at twelve sharp."

Wilfred watched the detective make a hasty exit and then turned back to Johnny. "You sure that was a good idea? Feller raced outta here like his pants was on fire and his hair was catchin'."

Peter laughed.

Johnny looked at the boy for a moment and then said, "Peter, why don't you go find your ma. See if she needs any help with anything. You got to sit in, but I think she's right. What me and Wilfred gotta talk about now don't nobody need to know just yet."

Peter's shoulders slumped. "So I'm not really in the posse."

"Listen, kid, you know more about this than almost everybody in town. But knowing stuff ain't always the safest. I ain't gonna leave you out, but we're both already on thin ice with your ma. If you're wanting to keep sitting in with Wilfred and I, you best make sure your ma don't feel like she's getting left out, neither."

"All right, all right," Peter scooted back his chair and walked out of the room, head hanging.

Wilfred waited till Peter was out of earshot and spoke. "Well?"

"Well," Johnny said, leaning across the table toward the man. "Do I think it was good idea to tell Phil? I certainly hope so. The man was right about one thing. The most important part of this is knowing where to look. He just had his sights on the wrong thing."

"You ain't looking for the gold?"

Johnny smiled and reached into a pocket. "I ain't lookin' for the gold currently, no. I already know where to find it." He tossed the folded map across to the deputy.

Wilfred opened the sheet and scanned the lines and directions. After a moment, a grin started to spread across his face. "When'd you find this?"

"Like I said," Johnny replied. "This afternoon. I just didn't happen to tell the rest of what I done."

"You made a copy?"

"Better," Johnny laughed.

Wilfred's eyes lit up as he grasped the plan. "You made a fake."

"Precisely," Johnny said. "Something about Phil hasn't set right with either of us, so now we'll give him a chance to prove us right or wrong. He knows where the map is ..."

"He knows where *a* map is," Wilfred interjected.

"Very true. He knows where a map is, and he knows that the clock is ticking. If he's going to go after it, he's gotta do it before noon tomorrow."

Wilfred sat for a moment, his smile fading slightly. "You know," he said. "He does have another option. He could just let us lead him to the gold and then kill us out in the scrub."

Johnny nodded slowly. "He could. But my gut is telling me, if they can get that gold, they ain't gonna waste any time getting as far away from here as they can."

"So the clock's ticking for us as well."

Johnny simply nodded again, though the look of satisfaction on his face was undeniable. "Fancy keeping an eye on the office for a few hours? Figured I'd come relieve ya later on."

Wilfred stood up with a sigh. "Wasn't planning on nothing fancy tonight anyway. Just sleepin', but I done that before.'"

***

Later that night, Johnny sat on the front porch, running through problems with the plan for the hundredth time. If Phil led them to Kansas, as he was almost sure the supposed detective would, they could hopefully nab the pair of them. Of course, that in and of itself was the biggest problem of all. Assuming everything went smoothly, he still had no idea how many men might be waiting when Phil and Kansas crossed paths.

From inside, the murmur of voices raised in pitch for a moment, a door slammed, and before Johnny could even get fully out of his chair, Etta burst through the front door, tears on her cheeks and a paper clutched in her hand.

"Whoa, hey, hey," Johnny was up immediately, holding the woman by the shoulders. "What's going on? It's too late in the day for there to be too much trouble."

"You're right about that," the woman said, her voice a mixture of anger, frustration, and sadness. "The trouble's been going on a while now and we didn't even know." She held the page out to Johnny.

He skimmed through the lines quickly. It was a letter from Peter's teacher, informing Etta that, due to Peter's current habit of "only attending when it seems to please him," in addition to his previous difficulties in "finding solutions to his problems with his words instead of his fists," he was no longer welcome at the schoolhouse.

"Should the situation right itself, he is welcome to begin again in the fall, though I suggest the upmost discipline and rigor in his upbringing over the ensuing months," Johnny finished reading. He looked at Etta and laughed.

"What's so funny?"

"Maybe he ain't so bad off," Johnny said. "I may not be the smartest fella in town, but even I know 'upmost' ain't a word."

Etta looked at him for a moment and then, with a sigh, fell into one of the chairs on the porch. "I'm glad you see the humor in all this. My son has ruined his future." She shot a look at Johnny. "Did you know about this? Tell me the truth."

Johnny folded the paper and sat back down in his chair. "You know I wouldn't approve of his lightin' out on his own. If I'da known, it woulda been because he was with me. You know that."

Etta wiped the angry tears from her cheeks with the back of her hand. "I know, I know. It wasn't fair to accuse you and I apologize. I'm just … I can't believe …"

Johnny waited for her to finish and, when she didn't, spoke up. "This may sound a little unorthodox, but if you want my opinion, given the way things've been going of late, maybe it's best he, and you, don't have his schoolin' to worry about. I know as well as anybody how you fret when he's down that way. Even before the rest of this mess got started. Seems to me this may be an opportunity. Let's get ourselves safe and settled, then we can get back to the normal ways."

Etta looked at him. "It's simple to say, isn't it?"

"Look," he replied. "You excused yourself from the meeting tonight, and that's perfectly understandable. But one thing you missed was that, in the next coupla days, this oughtta all behind us."

"Really?" Etta's voice held both hope and doubt in the one quiet word.

"Really," Johnny said. "Let me take care of this mess Peter got hisself into and then, well, what teacher could turn away a young man who missed his lessons on accounta he was helping the local sheriff?"

Etta gave him a wary look. "I'm not sure that sounds much better. How exactly do you see him helping?"

Johnny laughed. "I just meant I'll keep an eye on him. Seems to me he's gonna be runnin' off every chance he can. May as well keep him by my side where I know what he's up to."

"I don't know," Etta said.

"I promised you before, and I promise you now again, ain't nothing gonna happen to that boy while he's with me. And when it's said and done, I'll get him right back in that schoolroom where he belongs."

Etta looked out at the dark night for a few moments and then back to Johnny. "I don't know what it is about you," she said, standing up and walking back to the door. "It's like," she paused, putting a hand on his shoulder, "no matter what you say, no matter how much my mind tells me it's foolishness ... I trust you. I've never done that with someone before."

Johnny reached over and patted her hand gently. "That makes two of us." He let his hand rest on hers for a moment, the feeling of butterflies in his stomach.

"Just, whatever I may say, promise to keep me informed. And if I say no to something, you have to be on my side. Please. I only want what's best for him."

Johnny looked back over her shoulder at the woman. "Myself as well. I give you my word to keep you involved in this as much as I possibly can. I will make it my upmost priority."

Etta gave him a small smile, a quiet laugh and, squeezing his shoulder, went inside.

Chapter Thirty-Four

As midnight approached, across town in the dirty room serving as Dane Kansas's office for the moment, he looked across the desk at Phil Anderson, the crooked detective, and Jake, the young, eager protege.

Kansas had initially been pleased with what Phil had uncovered, especially since, after Phil had only been given what turned out to be useless papers from the sheriff, Kansas had been almost back to square one. Breaking into the sheriff's office in hopes of finding something was not nearly the type of plan he preferred to follow. Hoping never got a fella anywhere.

Unfortunately, the Pinkerton pretender was now beginning to show signs of unrest himself. It was something Kansas always anticipated, though after working with a familiar crew for so long, he hadn't had to deal with it in such a capacity. Coy was a fluke, an outlier. It wasn't natural for an outlaw to follow the path Coy did. Men like him were supposed to be fodder, die in a bank robbery, a shoot-out. They were expendable tools. To up and leave the gang, especially to leave the gang and then take on such a large score, well that was just unacceptable.

But he had been dealt with, at least the man had. To Kansas's frustration though, now that he was finally beginning to wrap up the loose ends with Coy, Anderson came in and, instead of being another useful tool, started to make problems with the machinery.

Kansas glanced across the desk at Jake. "Why don't you step outside for a few minutes? Me and Anderson got some talk that don't concern you."

"Sure thing, boss." The young man stood up and left the room.

Kansas let his eyes fall back on Anderson, purposefully letting the moment linger to an almost uncomfortable length.

"You see that there?" Kansas said finally, gesturing toward the door Jake had just exited.

"The kid?"

"The response."

Anderson looked behind him, then back at Kansas, and shrugged.

"I told the kid to leave, and he left." Kansas took off his hat and tossed it on the desk. "That's how things are supposed to work around here. I want something to happen; you all make it happen."

Anderson leaned back, crossing one leg over the other at the knee. "You sayin' I ain't doing that? You said get in with the sheriff. I did. You said find out where the map is. I did. And I did it darn fast and easy too, if you'd like my opinion on it."

Kansas scratched at his stubbly beard. "Interesting how you see it that way," he said. "I don't doubt for a second you think you done a good job of it. I'd even be inclined to say so myself, except for one thing. You're starting to think you done too good a job of it. See, the way I figure, I brung you in here to do a job. I offered you a fee and you agreed to it. What I can't understand is how you now sit here telling me, in front of that young man no less, that the fee you yourself agreed to ain't enough."

Anderson shrugged. "Prices go up. I come in here to do one thing, find out where that gold is. Next thing I know, you got me spending half my day with the law and the other half twiddlin' my thumbs in a boarding house cause even if ain't nobody around I still gotta act like I'm a daggone detective. This was supposed to be a quick job and it's been anything but. I think it's fair to get myself compensated for that."

"Ohhh," Kansas smiled. "So you're wanting a per diem, that it? Every day you hang out here the price just keeps going higher and higher?"

"Seems fair to me," the man said.

"Now, see, here we are again. That's interesting," Kansas folded his hands in his lap. "Because what it sounds like is, we had a deal, and now you want a new deal, even though the job hasn't changed at all. In fact, as you said, you were supposed to find out where the gold is. All right, Phil, where's the gold?"

Anderson threw his hands in the air. "You know I don't know that."

"But that was the job. Or so you just said."

"I know where the map is. That's the same thing. Like as near at least."

Kansas chuckled. "Like as near … You're the kinda fella who'd sell me a goat and call it a horse, ain't ya? It's got four legs, eats straw. Like as near a horse, huh?"

"You know it ain't like that," Anderson said, his voice growing frustrated. "All I'm saying is, what's it gonna hurt you to toss a little extra my way? You got your boy out there," he hitched a thumb at the door. "You both say there ain't nothing he can't break into. And I'm sitting here saying, all we gotta do is go pluck the journal out of the office. All the kid's gotta do is open the window. Shoot, I can just go break the thing out myself and be done with it."

Kansas leaned forward in his chair, his hands laced between his knees. "So we should cut the kid out? His job ain't necessary anymore?"

Anderson shrugged. "I ain't saying that. But I ain't *not* sayin' that either."

Kansas stood up and paced slowly around the room. The space was small, forcing him to look behind the desk and where Anderson was sitting. "Y'know," he said, walking behind the desk, his chin in his hand. "You may have a point. We get the journal. We get the map," he paused at the dusty window at the side of the building. The inky night showed him nothing but his own reflection. "We could have the gold and be gone before the sun comes up, if we so desired."

"That's the way I'd play it," Anderson said.

Kansas started walking again. "I'll give you this," he said, circling the room. "It ain't a half-bad idea. But," he stopped behind Anderson, putting a hand on the man's shoulder. "The thing is, I just *like* Jake better'n you." He felt the man tense. "So I reckon if anybody's reached the end of their use ..."

Kansas drew quickly, fluidly. It was a motion he'd done so many times the gun was fired and back in its holster before Anderson's body hit the floor. Smoke curled about in the still air of the room.

Behind him, the door opened quickly. Jake, his gun drawn, almost leapt inside.

"Everything all right?"

"Everything's fine," Kansas said. "Just a little misunderstanding, ya might say."

Jake looked at the body, putting his gun back in the holster.

"What have I always told you about cutting a deal?" Kansas said, kneeling down by Anderson but looking up at Jake.

"Make sure you get it right the first time 'cause there ain't no going back on it."

Kansas smiled. "Precisely. Anderson wanted to renegotiate. Problem is, he didn't have nothin' to bargain with."

"So what's the plan then?"

"Same as before," Kansas said. "You get into that office tonight, find the map, we'll come up with a plan tomorrow. Seems to me if Anderson here felt he could waste half the evening arguing, there can't be much rush."

"You need help with the body?"

Kansas thought for a second and then smiled. "Nah, I'll handle it. Warn't in the deal for me and you tonight."

Chapter Thirty-Five

Johnny sat in the sheriff's office alone. He'd come to relieve Wilfred of his watch around three in the morning but the man had been nowhere to be found. He knew Wilfred too well to think the man would've shirked his duties, but there was no sign of anything out of the ordinary either in or around the building.

Except for the missing journal.

Johnny stared down at the top of his desk. There could be no doubt who was behind it. Nothing in the office had been rooted through. No drawers were open, no files gone through. Even the door and windows had been securely locked.

He ran a hand through his hair. His body was tired. His mind was running a hundred miles an hour. If the gang had found Wilfred, they could've forced him to let them in. That would explain the lack of evidence of a break-in. It would also explain Wilfred's absence. But there should've been some signal, some clue, some *something.* Wilfred was too smart to have let himself be taken so easily.

But where else could he be?

There was no sense in riding out pell-mell, aimless. If the gang had Wilfred, Johnny hoped they at least had the good sense to try and ransom the man. Kidnapping a lawman was bad enough; if they murdered him, there wouldn't be a safe enough place in the nation for them to hide.

The sun was coming up outside when Johnny heard footsteps at the door of the office. At first he'd reached for his gun. Then, realizing the lightness, the short strides, he knew it could only be one person.

Peter opened the door and stepped inside. He had a basket in his hand, his head hanging low.

"Ma sent me here with breakfast. She said I'm to either stay with you or turn around and come back home, but I'm not to be trusted on my own."

Johnny looked at the boy. Peter was clearly repentant, though he had the feeling it wasn't due to the problems at school. The way the boy had mumbled the last few words had been more of embarrassment, of having to admit something less than complimentary to someone he admired. A small spark of pride shone in the sheriff's heart. The kid might not have his priorities exactly in order, but he at least wasn't bull-headed enough to think he didn't need anyone. Letting Johnny down might have been the kick in the pants the boy needed to straighten himself out.

"I appreciate it," Johnny said. "C'mon in and sit down."

Slowly, Peter walked over to the desk, sitting the food on its surface. "You want for me to get on back?" he asked quietly.

Johnny leaned forward and opened the basket, the smell of warm sausage wafting up. "You eat yet?"

"Yes, sir. With ma. She said if I warn't going to school, I needed to be working. So she had me help cook."

Johnny nodded. "That seem fair to you?"

Peter looked up at the man slightly. "To be honest, sir, I don't know. Part of me ... well, I guess I understand. She probably oughtta send me off to 'prenticeship somewhere. It's what boys do if they ain't cut out for school."

Johnny moved the basket to the side so he could see the youth across from him better. "You think you ain't cut out for school, huh? Gonna be awful hard to become a lawman if you ain't got no letters and numbers under your belt."

Peter shrugged. "Maybe that ain't in the cards for me. Lawman's gotta be responsible. Take care of people. I'm just letting folks down." He looked up at Johnny, then quickly away. "But I'm trying to help! I am! I didn't mean to cross paths with Kansas, but I didn't wanna just sit in that dumb school doing nothing while you was out looking for him. While he's out there. He might be after my ma!"

Johnny sat for a second, looking at the boy. "What were you doing when you skipped out on school them days?"

Peter sighed. "I was home. Well," he paused. "Not in the house. Outside. I was scared something would happen to Ma. Kansas is a smart fella. He can find out who I am. And if you're looking for him, and I'm at school, well, who says he wouldn't go after my ma instead? Nobody was there lookin' after her. Wilfred was with you. Anderson ..." he shrugged. "I don't mean to be rude, but I don't like that man so much anymore."

Johnny folded his arms across his chest. "You ain't wrong on that account, kid. But so you was home them days, keepin' an eye on your ma, huh?"

"Yes, sir. I figured if something happened well, I don't know ... but I had to look after her. It's just us two."

Johnny started to reply when heavier footfalls came rushing down the wooden sidewalk outside. There was no knock, no hesitancy, just Wilfred bursting through the front door of the office. "I found 'em!"

***

Johnny knew Etta wouldn't like it, but he didn't have the time to drop the boy back off at his house. And truth be told, even if he did, there was no guarantee the kid wouldn't slip out and try to track him down anyway. Maybe riding between Johnny and Wilfred wasn't the safest place in the world, but at least the sheriff could keep an eye on him.

Wilfred's explanation had been succinct, quick. If Johnny hadn't been so worn down, he would've seen the possibility himself, despite how unlikely it seemed at first. And in the end, he supposed, it made a strange kind of sense. Fellas like Kansas get a reputation, sure, but that was only good in certain instances. Outlaws like him, the ones who wanted to make a life out of it, they needed to go unnoticed far more often than not.

"Slickest thing I ever seen," Wilfred had said. "And I seen a lot. Kid had the window open in no time flat. Slipped in, grabbed the book, popped back out. I s'pose I coulda nabbed him then and there, tried to get him to spill what he knew. But seeing as how Anderson wasn't with him, I figured we had a few more things we needed to figure out.

"So, I hung back, followed him out this way to the shack they're holed up in. I tried to get up close as I could, but seeing as how I didn't know how many were in there, I didn't figure it'd do me much good gettin' caught on my own."

Johnny sat straight in the saddle, listening. "Makes sense," he said, after a moment. "What I woulda done too."

"Lemme ask you something though," Wilfred said as they rode. "Anything seem funny to you in there?"

Johnny sighed. "Just the fact that nothing seemed funny at all, I guess."

"That's what I thought," Wilfred replied. "Afore the kid took off, he pulled that window back closed again. Had hisself a little piece of metal with him he was working around the frame. I know that's how a fella can get in, but ..."

Johnny let out a single laugh. "Looks like that's how you keep the sheriff occupied too. He musta been locking the window back up. Way things looked inside, all I could figure was they'd had you unlock the front door for 'em."

"Ain't that clever," Wilfred said, almost to himself.

"Wait." It was Peter. He whispered quickly, holding a hand up. "That it?"

Johnny and Wilfred reined in their horses, looking through the hazy morning light to where the boy was pointing. If he strained his eyes, he could just make out the outline of a small building through the trees.

"You got eyes like a cat, kid," Wilfred said. "Oughtta leave the horses here, I reckon."

The old man dismounted, followed by the sheriff and Peter.

"This ain't a joke now," Johnny said to Peter. "Games are long behind us. I know I ain't gotta tell you that, but my only options are to leave you here or take you with us. I figure you seen Kansas one too many times on your own as it is. But you do like you done on the trail. If you ain't behind me or Wilfred, you're in the wrong place." He paused, then added somberly, "And if I tell you to run, you don't take a second to look back. Got it?"

Peter nodded.

Johnny was thankful the boy didn't ask any questions because, truth be told, the sheriff wasn't sure he'd have the answers.

The trio crept up through the underbrush, a few feet between them. A few tendrils of smoke wafted lazily from the chimney, but otherwise, the place was motionless, quiet. Keeping low, Wilfred crept over to the other two.

"Had their horses tied up over yonder," he said, pointing to a small tree by the front door of the shack. "I don't know if this is just a way-station or if this is the main hideout, but if I had to guess, there ain't nobody in there right now."

Johnny glanced back and forth around the building. A small dirt path led up to it, but there didn't seem to be any other approaches to the building. One way in, one way out. It wasn't ideal in a lot of situations, but for the sheriff, it was about the best he could hope for.

"All right," he said. "Peter, you stay here with Wilfred. Keep your ears open."

Johnny slipped up through the foliage, moving as quietly as he could on the soft earth. If there were men inside, the last thing he needed was a cracking branch or a kicked stone to give him away.

The place had certainly seen better days. Scraggly underbrush grew up tall and unhindered around all points on the building except for the small path out front. The shack itself seemed to have a kind of lean to it, as if it were on its way to falling over, but taking its sweet time about it. Along the ground, where the walls met the earth, a few dark holes could be seen, either dug as burrows into what he presumed was a small cellar, or places where the rain had begun to wash away at the underside of the building.

He made a quick circuit of the building, glancing in the dirty windows as well as he could, and then came back around to the front porch. He stood silently at the corner of the shack a moment longer, listening, then gestured toward where Wilfred and Peter waited.

As the other two crept up to the front, Johnny tried the front door.

"You're kidding me," he said under his breath as the door swung open.

"Reckon they didn't figure nobody'd find this place," Wilfred said, stepping up on the porch. "Or they're just plain stupid."

"Maybe a little of both," Johnny said, stepping into the gloomy room. "But I reckon they aren't planning on staying here too long. Besides, see the rust on that hardware? This door hasn't shut proper in ages. Why bother fixing up a place you ain't planning on hanging around?"

Bringing up the rear, Peter sneezed once, twice.

"Little dusty, ain't it?" Wilfred said.

"No," Peter got down on his hands and knees, looking under the table and an off-kilter bed in the corner. "There you are."

Johnny watched as the kid leaned under the bed, making coaxing noises, finally pulling a scrawny calico cat out from the darkness. He sneezed again. The cat, spooked, jumped from his arms and ran under the kitchen table and out onto the porch, disappearing around the corner of the house.

"Allergic," Peter said, shrugging. "I like dogs better anyway."

"Over here," Wilfred said, drawing Johnny's attention away from the boy.

The deputy stood at the small table which seemed to be serving double-duty as a desk as well. A few papers were stacked in the corner, but taking the center space was Coy's journal, Johnny's fake map spread out next to it.

"Looks like they took the bait," the deputy said.

"Perfect." Johnny sorted through a few of the other sheets. "Looks like they left us some surprises too." He held up a sheet. "Receipts. Orders. Moonshine, guns, gals ... Old Kansas may be a cold-hearted fella, but he's organized about it."

Wilfred walked over and leafed through a few of the pages on the table. "All this, we don't even need Coy's murder to keep him locked up for good."

"No," Johnny said. "But no sense in leaving any loose ends."

The sheriff cocked his head to the side and then raced over to the window. Taking a quick glance outside, he hurriedly pushed the front door closed again, his eyes searching the room rapidly.

"What is it?" Peter asked, his voice instinctively a whisper.

"They're coming back," Wilfred said. The deputy moved up to the window, staying low while Johnny scanned the floor.

"What do we do?" Peter's eyes were wide, his hands moving aimlessly, the motions of someone who knew he needed to do something, but had no earthly idea what.

"Here," Johnny said, reaching down. The latch had been on the wall side, almost hidden in the gloom. "The cellar."

Wilfred glanced over at him. "Not many ways out of there."

"No," Johnny said, "but we ain't got a lot of choices here neither. C'mon."

Chapter Thirty-Six

The floorboards creaked overhead and dust danced in the few shafts of light that made their way into the small earthen hiding place. Johnny had instinctively moved Peter to the far side of the cramped space, keeping him back in the corner least likely to be seen by someone coming down the short, steep staircase.

Wilfred stood on one side of the boy, Johnny on the other. The dirt floor muffled their movements, what small steps they would allow themselves, and the raucousness of the men above drowned out any other telltale sounds.

"Here, kitty kitty," they heard one of the men say, the sound of boots making its way back and forth above them. The cellar only accounted for about a third of the space under the floor, but it was enough for them to track the men fairly well. More importantly, it allowed them to hear the outlaws.

"Told you that thing was gonna run off."

Johnny looked at Wilfred, his eyebrows up.

The deputy shrugged. It was nearly impossible to identify any of the men without seeing them.

"I tell ya," they heard a man say. "I ain't sayin' we didn't need to get rid of that Anderson fella, but that's the last time I spend all morning digging a hole after spending all night at the saloon. I'm sweating like a stuck pig."

"Consequences of celebrating too early," a different man said. "Besides, you've barely done your part. Jake here was the one who got the map."

"Oh I ain't even begun to celebrate yet," the first man said. "But if there's more diggin' to be done, I aim to get me some shut-eye before that happens." A flump from upstairs indicated the fellow had let himself fall down on the dirty bed.

"Get your boots off there," the second voice said, gruffly. "Bedrolls for the two of you."

An exasperated sigh came from the far end of the house. "I didn't know you was planning on sticking around." The floorboards creaked again as the man stood up.

"Until the rest of the crew gets here, I think the three of us would be wise to lay low. Besides," boots crossed to the table that was almost directly above the three, "I don't plan on leaving this lay about. From this point on, we're sticking together."

"When you wanna make our move?"

Johnny glanced at Wilfred again, earning him yet another shrug. It was a new voice, younger. The deputy had said the one who broke into the office had been a youth.

The heavy footfalls crossed the room from the table to where the bed was situated. "Reckon the rest of the boys oughtta be here by tonight, tomorrow morning at the latest. I'd say by tomorrow night, we oughtta have our hands on it."

One of the men whistled. "Lotta money just sitting there waiting on us."

"And it can wait another day," the man, the one Johnny assumed was the leader, and therefore very likely Dane Kansas said.

"I reckon."

There was a scuffle of boots and blankets above as the three men arranged themselves for a very late chance at sleep.

Johnny leaned over and whispered to Peter and Wilfred. "Give him a little time to nod off, then we get out of here."

Peter looked at him and mouthed one word. "How?"

***

The longer the three stood in the cellar, the more Johnny started to believe that only a clear conscience made for a good night's sleep. The men above were restless, talking in their sleep, moving about. Initially, Johnny had hoped to move within half an hour at most. If the men had truly been up all night carousing, and then likely out burying the fake detective, surely they should've dropped right off. He hoped Peter was too caught up in the moment to ponder just what had kept the outlaws occupied all evening.

As it was, it was over an hour before the somewhat rhythmic snores became consistent enough he felt comfortable starting their escape.

"All right," he said, just barely breathing out the words. "Now's our chance."

"We can't go back up," Wilfred said.

"I know," Johnny replied. He pointed into the gloomy corner where the wall and ceiling met. At first it had been hazy, but as their eyes adjusted to the light, he'd become more and more certain it was their best bet.

"Ain't no way," the old man said.

"I'll go first," Johnny said. "I can draw them out, then you and Peter come up through the house."

"What if they don't all go?" Peter whispered. His voice wasn't frantic, which was good. It did have a strain to it, though, that underscored the seriousness of the situation. That was even better.

"Oh they'll come," Johnny grinned. "Getting the drop on 'em oughtta be enough on its own, but wakin' 'em up will make it even more of a mess."

He heard Wilfred sigh.

"You gotta trust me," Johnny said. "If it don't work, I reckon you can catch up on some sleep yourself. They ain't the only ones who had a long night."

Wilfred shook his head. "If we're gonna do this, let's do it."

"All right," Johnny said. "That burrow there oughtta come out just at the corner of the porch. I'll slip around to the far side of the building, draw 'em my way. Once you hear 'em come after me, it's up the stairs and out the front door. Get back to the horses and head for town. Don't bother waiting around; I'll be all right."

"There's three of 'em," Peter whispered.

"Yeah, but they don't know how many they're up against," Johnny smiled. "Ready?"

Wilfred went down on a knee, making a stirrup with his hands. Johnny unhooked his holster belt, wrapped it around the guns, and held them ahead of him. Then he stepped up and, with a bit of maneuvering, began to wriggle out through the soft earth, pushing the revolvers ahead of him.

It wasn't a far crawl, but it was tight. And for one brief moment, he felt himself get hung up on a root, or perhaps the underside of a foundation beam. Whatever it was, with the sound of tearing fabric, he was able to free himself and in almost no time, was lying on his stomach in the sunshine.

So far, so good.

He hunched down low and made his way to the opposite corner of the building, unraveling the gunbelt and cinching it around his waist again as he moved. If it weren't for the kid, this wouldn't have been so bad. At the same time, what was he supposed to do with him? Better to keep Peter somewhere that he was half under control than have him wandering up to the shack on his own.

At the far side of the shack he used the natural blindspot of its corner to move back into the underbrush, finding a bit of cover behind a fallen tree. He unholstered his guns and took a deep breath.

"C'mon boys!" Johnny shouted. "They're in the shack!"

He fired both his guns rapidly, hooting and hollering, hoping to give the impression it was more than just one fool out in the woods making a spectacle of himself. If he ever needed confusion to work in his favor, now was the time. Just to drive the point home, he fired a few bullets into the side of the shack, high, almost to the roofline. It would be impossible for the shots to do anything but give away which direction he was firing from, but that was really the only goal.

Johnny rushed back and forth, making as much noise as possible in the bushes and leaves, firing in the air and, with a grim smile, it was only moments before the front door of the shack burst open and the three men came tumbling out, guns drawn.

The sheriff fired into the dirt ahead of them, again into the roof of the building and then, once they seemed to focus in on where he was, began to move. The volley of gunfire that came back tore through empty space. Johnny was already on the move, running at an angle through the trees, firing back without aiming, hoping the sound would be enough to draw the men on.

Within a moment, he saw the first come around the corner of the house, rapidly followed by the other two. He glanced back toward the front porch, which was now completely obscured from the outlaws. With a sigh of relief, he saw Peter and Wilfred race off toward the woods, the deputy pausing only long enough to toss a quick glance back over his shoulder and bend down to the ground for a moment

Johnny fired until the hammers fell on empty shells and then broke into a sprint, hoping to meet Wilfred and Peter at the horses and make a quick getaway before the outlaws realized they were heading in the wrong direction.

Up ahead, he saw Wilfred boost Peter into saddle, practically throwing him onto the horse. The deputy might be getting older, but he could still move when he needed to.

Johnny burst through the underbrush and sprung onto his horse without breaking stride. "Everybody ..." he looked at Wilfred. "All right?"

The deputy had the calico cat under one arm. "Ain't leaving her with them yahoos."

Despite the situation, Johnny felt a grin coming to his lips. "Whatever you say, Wil. Let's move. We ain't got much time before–"

"This way! They come around on us!"

"Before that," Johnny finished, glancing back over his shoulder.

"I know a place!" Peter said quickly. "Unless you think we can outrun 'em."

Johnny exchanged a quick glance with Wilfred. "Lead the way, then, kid."

Chapter Thirty-Seven

Johnny stood in the ankle-deep water, watching as the three gang members rode full speed across the meadow and away from them.

"You done good, Pete."

The boy had handled the situation with the assurance and near-pleasure of any other afternoon adventure. Rather than heading immediately back toward town, Peter had led Johnny and Wilfred about twenty yards back into the woods and then made a hard turn, doubling back. The horses' hooves had skittered on the loose rock, but the decline had been brief and none-too-steep, just enough to get them out of the eyeline of their pursuers.

Peter had set his horse to a run across a small stream and toward what, for all Johnny could guess, was a stone wall. At the last moment, the boy had made a brushing gesture with his hand, waving away a thin curtain of mossy, overhanging growth.

Inside the small cave it was cool, dim. The moss made for perfect camouflage while still allowing Johnny to keep an eye on the gang members as they rode off on the wrong trail.

He turned to Peter. "You find this on one of your days away from school?"

Peter looked down and shook his head.

Johnny laughed. "Remind me to tell your teacher that when I talk to her. You may've missed a day on state's history, but you just saved a couple lives."

Peter looked up at him slowly, a proud smile spreading on his face.

"We're safe for the moment," Wilfred said, his hat almost touching the top of the cave from where he sat in the saddle. "What's next though? They ain't gonna stay gone forever."

"No," Johnny said, "and from the sound of things, the longer we wait the more of 'em there's gonna be. I say we sit tight for a minute, let 'em get a lead on us." He looked over at Peter. "This is the same creek come in the corner of town, ain't it?"

The boy nodded. "Eventually. Kinda meanders a ways."

"Good," Johnny said. "The less it seems like we're coming from this way, the better."

***

As they approached Johnny's home, he couldn't shake the feeling that something wasn't right. Part of his mind insisted it was the weather. The sunny morning had turned to an overcast midday, the skies seeming to threaten a heavy storm, but the rain never quite coming.

Perhaps he was just tired, as well, he thought. He'd been functioning on only a few hours of sleep. He glanced over at Wilfred who, though he would never admit it, had quite possibly mastered the skill of falling asleep in the saddle. The man never seemed to be completely asleep, though. "Resting his eyes," is how Wilfred always put it, but sometimes Johnny wondered if that was all the man needed. More than once on a long ride the deputy had surprised him by making a comment on their surroundings while having ridden in perfect silence, with seemingly shut eyes, for a good long time. Not for the first time, Johnny grinned to himself, wondering if Wilfred would be the one taking on the sheriff job when Johnny got ready to retire. The man just kept plugging along.

It was Peter, though, whose keen youthful eyesight finally picked out what it was that had been playing at the back of Johnny's mind, hinting at something being just slightly off.

"That looks like smoke," the boy said, breaking what had been a long silence.

He was pointing straight ahead. Johnny followed the youth's outstretched arm and his stomach sank. Before Peter could even finish his next sentence, Johnny had spurred his horse into a gallop.

Wilfred, almost preternaturally, opened his eyes and was on the move. "C'mon kid!" Johnny heard the older man yell.

After that, his senses shut out everything but what was in front of him. Peter was right, and Johnny should've noticed it. No amount of fatigue or bad weather should've shut out what was right in front of him. And now, as if the boy's words had brought it into being, there could be no doubt about what he was seeing.

It was smoke. And it was coming from Johnny's own property.

He led the three of them across the intervening pasture, splashing through a small creek, the horse leaping a half-fallen fence marking the long-forgotten boundary of someone's fields. Johnny barely noticed the motion beneath him. His only thoughts were on his home, and more importantly, the woman who had still been in that home this morning.

Johnny leapt from the horse almost before it had stopped moving. His hands instinctively went for the butts of his revolvers but his mind quickly assessed the situation, stopping him.

There were people about, to be sure. But they weren't the Kansas gang. They were his neighbors. The ramshackle volunteer firefighters had already formed in a bucket brigade, dowsing what remained of the flaming timbers. Johnny raced for the house, ignoring the calls of recognition from the townspeople in his yard.

It was just the barn. It was something he'd worked on himself over the years, putting his sweat and blood into it, but now, it was just a building. He allowed himself only a slight relief when he saw the house appeared to be untouched.

By flames, at least.

The front door hung askew, only the bottom hinge keeping the wood in place. Johnny bounded up onto the porch and into the house. A pair of ladies were standing in the kitchen, clearly at a loss for what to do.

Giving them only a cursory look, Johnny rushed into his bedroom.

There, on the bed, lay Etta.

Doc Watts was perched on a stool beside her, running a wet cloth over her forehead and then ringing it out again in a basin of water that bore a sickening red hue. A large gash split the skin across her temple from her hairline to the bottom of her eye.

"How is she?" The words were more of a demand than a question.

Watts turned and, seeing the sheriff, held a finger to his lips. He put the cloth back in the water, the basin on the floor, and led Johnny out into the main room of the cabin.

Just then, Wilfred and Peter came through the door.

"Where's my ma?" Peter raced toward the bedroom.

Johnny hooked the kid with an arm and pulled him tightly to his side. "She's resting, Pete. Doc here was just gonna tell us that, weren't ya?" He eyed the man somberly.

"Yes, yes," Watts said, seeming more convinced of his words than Johnny had at first hoped. The basin seemed to be brimming with blood to his eyes. "Let's sit for a moment."

"I'll stand," Johnny said, the nervous energy in his body making any kind of repose impossible.

"I'll go help with the brigade," Wilfred said, excusing himself to almost no one.

Watts sat on one of the wooden chairs at the side of the room and wiped his glasses on a handkerchief.

"Like the sheriff said," Watts started, looking mostly at Peter. "Your ma will be just fine. She got a bit of a knock on the head, but she's all right. I come here soon as I heard the ruckus and got her cleaned up and laid down comfortable. Be best if you don't bother her right now, but I'll come get you shortly and take you in."

Peter looked between the doctor and Johnny.

The sheriff understood the doctor's message as well as the boy's pleading, but couldn't risk Etta's safety any more than he already had. How could he have been so foolish as to leave her alone? Even the boy'd had more sense than him. He was letting his own pride get in the way, the chase after Kansas, the idea of saving the day, being the hero.

He felt disgusted with himself.

"Go on," he said to Peter. "Get out there and help Wilfred. I'll come get ya."

Peter's eyes flared momentarily, but even frustrating the boy couldn't cut through the remorse Johnny already felt at his own blindness to the situation.

As Peter stomped off out the front door, Johnny turned to Watts. "How bad is it?"

"Despite what you might be inclined to believe, what I told the boy was mostly true. Etta did take a blow to the head, though I don't have any reason to believe it was an accident."

"Yeah," Johnny said shortly. "The barn kinda tipped me off on that."

"The barn might be the best thing that happened," Watts said, his voice calm. "Smoke brought the neighbors. Neighbors brought me."

"Anyone see who done it?" The question felt pointless even as Johnny asked it.

"No, but judging by the looks of Etta's injuries, she put up a fight against whoever it was. I'm not trying to do your job here, but if I had to guess, the barn was what saved her. Whoever was in here with her likely had to leave prematurely. She was dealt a solid blow to the temple with a blunt object, hard enough to break the skin, knocking her unconscious. Now, I was able to move her and get her cleaned up, but she'll need her rest."

Johnny thought for a moment. What the man said made sense. If the three who had chased them had already figured out who they were chasing, coming back here made the most sense. Two, even one, could've roughed up Etta while the remainder lit the barn. Thankfully, the old wood took the flames fast.

"What else?" he looked at the doctor, who shrugged.

"There is nothing else," Watts said, standing up. "Let her rest. Tend to your barn, the boy. She'll pull through if you just give her time. Say what people will about that young woman, but she's a fighter."

"How long, doc?"

"That," the doctor sighed, "I'm afraid I don't know."

Chapter Thirty-Eight

Johnny sat with Peter in the bedroom, Etta lying quietly in front of them. The barn had already been mostly dealt with by the time the three had returned from their experience at the cabin, and other than giving his thanks, Johnny had had little use for the folks lingering about his yard.

Leaving Wilfred in charge of the office and the crowd control, Johnny had brought Peter back inside to see his mother for the first time.

Before leaving, Doc Watts had bandaged her head with clean cloths, carefully wiping the last streaks of blood from her cheek and brow. If it weren't for the wrapping, one could almost believe the woman was sleeping naturally.

Peter had entered the room hesitantly, almost as if the sound of his footsteps alone could be detrimental to his mother's condition. He'd sat where the doctor had been when Johnny first arrived, in almost the exact same position of concern. Slowly, Peter had reached out and taken her hand. Then, for the longest time, the two had just sat in silence, watching the woman rest.

"What did he really say?" Peter asked after a time. "I know I'm a kid, but I deserve to know."

Johnny sighed. "The honest truth is that he told me about the same thing he told you."

"About the same, or the same? Someone did this to her, didn't they?"

"That seems to be the look of it," Johnny said.

"The men from the cabin? Kansas and them?"

"Ain't nobody seen who done it for sure, but if I was to take a guess, that'd be it."

"I should've stayed," Peter said, almost echoing Johnny's thoughts about himself. "If I had just come back after seeing you this morning, I woulda been here."

"That's true," Johnny said.

Peter looked at him, then, after a moment, sniffed. "And then you'd have two of us laid up, wouldn't you?"

"Maybe," Johnny said. "Maybe not. Maybe I'd have two of you dead. Maybe I wouldn't have anybody here at all. Maybe don't do us much good in life, Pete. What we got is what we gotta deal with."

The boy looked back at his mother, apparently chewing on the sheriff's words.

"It's still my fault," Peter said finally. "If I hadn't run off that day, I'da never been out there when Kansas killed Coy. I'da never gotten involved. Ma and I woulda been just fine."

"Could be," Johnny agreed. "Or it could be things would've turned out worse. If you hadn't been out that day, we wouldn't've crossed paths either. I know things haven't been easy, and I'd give anything to have your ma back feeling fine, but I for one am glad me and you crossed paths." He paused, letting out a small laugh. "But I gotta agree with you on one thing, the circumstances coulda been a little better."

Peter looked at him. "It ain't funny."

"I ain't saying it is. But you wanna start casting blame about, you're looking at the wrong fella in this room. I don't see a star pinned to your shirt. I don't see a gun on your hip. My job, my whole reason for being in this community, is to make sure folks keep in line. I'm supposed to help. I'm supposed to look out for y'all. Now this, this was right in my own home.

"We can sit here all day and come up with ways this coulda been prevented. I coulda sent you back. I coulda sent Wilfred back with you. I coulda gone out and got half the men in this town who'da been willing to try and track down Kansas with me. But I didn't. We got a whole city to blame if we want to. We can sit here and blame ourselves, or we can be thankful it ain't any worse than it is. I don't know about you, but the only one that seems any good to me is the last one."

Peter lapsed into another long silence. Etta's slow breathing was the only sound in the room. Johnny saw the boy reach up and surreptitiously wipe at his cheek.

"I ain't caused her nothing but trouble, since the day I was born," he said quietly. "And now this. If she don't make it, Johnny ..." his voice hitched.

The sheriff leaned over and put a hand on the boy's shoulder. "She's gonna make it," he said. "And I guess that's one thing you didn't hear the doc say after all. He told me, hand to God, she's one of the strongest women he knows, and that's what makes the difference. The person's gotta want to pull through; they gotta have a reason to fight. You say what you will about yourself and problems you think you may've caused, but you're her reason to fight. You're the reason she wants to pull through. This woman right here loves you fiercely, Peter. No matter what you think, you best not doubt that."

"I just wish ..." Peter wiped at his eyes again.

"We all wish a lotta things," Johnny said softly. "Lord knows I got a list a mile long of things I wish were different. But who knows? Maybe if I wished for one thing, I'd lose something else. This is where we are right now. It ain't always pretty, but I'm choosing to see the good in it."

Peter rubbed his thumb back and forth on his mother's hand. "That may be," he said after a moment, "but let me ask you something."

"What's that?"

"Can I see the good in it, and still be mad?"

Johnny squeezed the boy's shoulder. "Son," he said. "I'm ready to spit fire. You be as mad as you'd like. Cause we ain't done yet."

Chapter Thirty-Nine

The next morning, Johnny sat in his office, Doc Watts's words still ringing in his ears.

Infected ... needs more care ... delicate ... time ...

The woman hadn't awoken during the night, though her dreams – and Johnny's as well, as he sat in the chair at her bedside – had been fitful. Peter, curled up at the foot of the bed, had at least given in to the exhaustion of the long and strenuous day. Johnny felt like he'd never sleep properly again, at least not until Etta was on her feet again.

Doc Watts had tried to be hopeful, but the concern in his voice was blatant. If things got worse, they were going to have to move her to a bigger city. If the infection really took hold, they would have to move fast, but even then, the fastest horses might not be enough. He promised to check in multiple times, administering whatever medication he could, changing bandages, monitoring her breathing and heart, but for the moment, they were in limbo.

He tried to get Peter to come into the office with him, not so much to keep an eye on the boy but to keep the youth's mind occupied. To his surprise, though, Peter had refused. He said he wanted to stay by his mother, have Watts show him what to do in case anything needed done. Watts had seen no problem with it, even commended the boy for his dedication, but that left Johnny to worry on his own.

Thankfully, Wilfred had been hard at work.

In the office with him, besides the deputy, were half a dozen lawmen from the surrounding towns. It wasn't exactly a militia, but it was a far sight better than one distracted sheriff and one elderly deputy.

"I want to thank y'all for doing this," Johnny said, forcing himself to focus on the task at hand. "I know y'all got your own towns and your own folks to look after, and I don't want you to think for a moment I won't remember this. Any of you ever need anything, you send word my way and I'll be there in a flash."

He looked around the room. The men, standing, sitting, perched on the corner of his desk even, nodded. They were a good posse, ready to take orders, not looking to do anything other than complete their duty. It was precisely what he needed. There was tension in the room; he could feel it. But it was the same low hum of indignation that any good man would've felt in this situation. Someone was out there, creating a threat to their homes and families, and whatever it took, this small group was willing to stand up and fight for it.

"I don't know how much Wilfred filled ya in on, so I apologize if some of this is repeat," Johnny said. "But so we're all on the same page, this is where we stand. Somewhere out there, we got Dane Kansas and at least two other men. They already killed two men we know of, attacked another female citizen, and burned down my barn.

"The son of this woman is also on Kansas's radar. Up until yesterday, I felt fairly sure the identity of this young man was unknown to anyone but myself and the deputy, but given present circumstances, I'm inclined to believe that's changed."

"I heard Pinkerton was in on this," one of the younger deputies spoke up.

Johnny smiled grimly. "Yeah, that's what a lot of folks would've liked to believe. Turns out the only ones who were unaware of that was the Pinkerton boys themselves. Our 'detective' was somehow associated with the Kansas gang. However, it would seem that Dane decided to end that partnership. While he was here, the man went by the name Phil Anderson. Whether that's his real name or not, I don't know, and frankly, at the moment, I don't much care.

"This may not be the way some of you were trained to do things, and if that's the case, I apologize for putting you in a tough spot. We get through here and any of ya feel like heading home, I ain't gonna fault ya none for it. You showed up. That says an awful lot right there."

He surveyed the room. Not a man moved. All eyes were still on him, calm, awaiting instruction.

"We got three places we need covered," Johnny continued. "In order of proximity, they'll be my house, a shack out on the edge of town, and here," he spread out his false map on the desktop. "Kansas has reason to believe the gold he's after, that from the Wells-Fargo robbery a few years back, is here," he pointed to the paper.

"I remember hearing about that," one of the men said. "What makes him think it'd turn up there all the sudden?"

"Well," Johnny said, "for one thing, the man who stole it, Coy McDill, was Kansas's first victim. Apparently Coy was the one who actually got away with the gold, and Kansas didn't take to not having it so well. The other reason he's headed here, I reckon, is on accounta I may've sorta told him it was there."

There was a murmur amongst the men.

"Not in so many words," Johnny said. "McDill did have a map, just like Kansas suspected. But I found it first. Replaced the real map with a copy like the one you see here, and let Kansas think he was stealing the genuine article."

A few chuckles bubbled up.

"Be honest, I thought it was a little amusing myself," Johnny said, allowing himself a small smile. "But that was before yesterday. 'Bout twenty-four hours ago, the deputy and myself found ourselves out at the cabin the gang's been holing up in. Seeing as how we were outnumbered, in addition to the fact that Kansas had made clear he had more men on the way, we decided to pull back and wait to make our move when the gang went for the gold. It's the only time I can reckon they'll all be in the same place at the same time.

"Unfortunately, we didn't slip out quite as smoothly as we'd like. They gave pursuit and, while we did get away, they musta figured out who we were. I come home to what ya might call a less than pleasant surprise. Which is why some of you, soon as we leave here, are heading to my house, where you'll stay until I personally come up and tell ya otherwise."

"Well, there's eight of us," one of the men said. "How you wanna divvy it up?"

"Any of y'all come together?"

A few hands raised, heads nodded.

"That's how we'll do it then. You two, you'll head to my house immediately. If he ain't there now, there'll be a doctor coming to tend to the woman. You talk to him if you need anything. Otherwise, keep your eyes open. I'll be coming your way later on.

"You three," he pointed to a group gathered in one corner of the room. "You're to head to the cabin. Wilfred here can tell ya how to get there. Odds are, by the time ya get there, the place'll be empty, but I suggest ya approach with all caution. Look for anything you can inside. If you don't see nothin', check the cellar. Who knows what you might find there."

To the puzzlement of most in the room, Wilfred let out a small laugh.

"That means me, Wilfred, and you, friend," he pointed to the only man who'd come on his own, "will head to the treasure hunt. Any questions?"

The men passed a few glances back and forth, and then stood in silence.

"Good. Wilfred, you tell these boys how to get where they're going. You two, I reckon you might as well come with me."

***

Johnny rode slowly around the remains of the barn, a deputy on either side of him. "As you can see, there' ain't much to block your visibility in any direction. Least not now that they cleared out the barn for ya. The cabin's roughly back that way," he pointed off in the distance behind them, "but this Kansas is a slippery fella. I wouldn't bank on him doing anything the same way twice."

"He passed through Mount Vernon a few years back," the one man said. "I'da been just as happy to never deal with him again."

"Lawrence county boys, are ya?" Johnny said.

"Yes, sir," the second answered. "Well, he's born and bred. I come up by way of Forsyth." He laughed a little to himself. "My adventure into the wild west didn't get me too far."

Johnny smiled. "Plenty wild enough right here for me. Hopefully you'll find this to be a properly boring day for ya."

As they crossed the yard, Doc Watts came out onto the porch, waving a hand at the sheriff.

"That'd be the doc there," Johnny said. "He's likely to be in and out, but you can trust him."

"If it's all the same to you, we may take another ride around the grounds here," the Forsyth man said. "Make sure we aren't missing anything."

Johnny nodded. "Have at it. I'll be inside."

As the two turned their horses, Johnny dismounted and walked up to Watts.

The man was nearly beaming. "She's up."

"Can I ...?"

"Go, go," Watts made brushing gestures with his hands. "I've been sent to find you and Peter. Looks like you were in the right place."

Ignoring the rest of what Watts could've possibly said, Johnny rushed into the house and back into the bedroom. There, propped up on pillows, the sheets up around her waist, Etta sat, a somewhat embarrassed smile on her face.

"Etta."

She glanced at him, then down at her hands. "You know, it's funny. Almost."

"What?"

"Well the other day, when you ... surprised me in the bath ... I thought that would be the most embarrassed I could be. This ..." she held her hands out, indicating her general situation, "this feels so much worse."

Johnny took the chair beside the bed, leaning in. "What could you possibly have to be worried about?" He grinned. "You've been sleeping; we've been the one worrying."

"You're going to make me feel worse," she said.

"Feel any way you want to feel. I'm just glad you can tell me about it. You gave me a real scare there."

Realizing the bluntness of his words, Johnny sat back in the chair a bit, trying to regain his professional composure. "How are you feeling?"

"Well," she sighed, "I've got one monster of a headache. My stomach's upset, but the doctor says that's on account of the medicine ... was it really so bad? Everyone acts like I'm back from the dead."

"Any kind of bad is too much bad in this case, I'd say."

Etta looked at him, trying to read his face. "Johnny," she said, her head to the side. "Can I ask you something?"

"Of course."

"I know it's not my business, but, well, these last few weeks. This," she held up her hands again, "whatever this is. I ... I guess I want to thank you, but that seems like so little. It's just your job. That's what I keep telling myself, but I don't know." She sighed. "Sometimes I think it's not just your job, that you're becoming a part of our lives, and that maybe we're becoming a part of yours. But then I think, I don't even know you. I mean. You're the sheriff, of course you look out for us."

He shook his head. "I think it's debatable about how good I'm doing at that."

She laughed a little. "The point is, you've done more for me and Peter than I ever imagined someone being willing to do and, well, I feel like I want to be completely honest with you about something, before anything else starts running around my mixed up mind."

Johnny looked at her.

"I suppose you already know," she said, her eyes darting around the room, as if there were a spot to look at that would somehow make this easier. "But, Peter's father. I ..." her voice hitched and she took a deep breath, apparently trying to settle herself. "I was attacked," she said finally.

Johnny reached over and put a hand on hers. She was right. He did know, or at least he knew enough from his years as a lawman to have pieced some things together. But still, there was nothing pleasant about having his idea confirmed.

"I don't know what I did," she said, her eyes starting to water. "I've never known what to do. I ... I try my best for Peter. But, the way the other boys tease him. The things people say. I feel like he must know but, at the same time, how do you tell a boy you don't even know who his father is?"

There was a gasp from the doorway. Johnny turned in time to see a flash as Peter disappeared into the main room. The front door slamming closed behind him.

Chapter Forty

Before she could speak, Johnny turned back to Etta. "I'll handle this. Your job right now is to rest, but I'm giving you another one. You have to trust me. Stay calm. I'll make it right."

Etta, her face in her hands, burst into sobs.

Johnny squeezed her shoulder. "It'll be okay. I'm sending the doc in."

The sheriff rushed through the house, almost stumbling over the doctor as he scanned the horizon for Peter.

"That way," the man pointed.

"Thanks," Johnny lingered on the porch for a moment. "Listen, go stay with her. Keep her calm. I don't know when we'll be back, but we will be. Make sure she knows that."

The doctor nodded and disappeared into the house.

Out in the pasture, Johnny could just make out the form of Peter running through the grass, away from the house. He jogged over to his horse and mounted, waving to the two deputies over by the barn. "I'll be back after a while. Y'all are in charge now."

The men waved back and Johnny turned the horse toward Peter's trail.

The lad was quick, there was no doubt about that, and the anger and frustration fueling his feet only added to the speed. But the energy granted by such emotions is quickly run down, even if the feelings continue long after. Johnny trotted the horse up to where the boy lay in the grass, his arm over his eyes, his body shaking.

Johnny looked down at him for a moment. Things could go so many ways. He'd never been prepared to have a son. His own father had always known what to say, and when to say nothing. If he had just had the old man around longer, if he'd been there now, Johnny would know the right questions to ask.

The sheriff looked at the youth in the grass, feeling himself hurt for the boy, feeling the temptation of following the what-ifs and maybes, just as he'd instructed Peter not to do.

"Peter," he said.

The boy rolled away from him, his arm still over his eyes.

"Peter, I ain't gonna sit here and tell you what you just heard was easy. I ain't gonna try and sweeten the news and I ain't gonna lie to you either. I got a job to do, and I intend to do it." He paused. "And the same goes for you."

The boy rolled back slightly, one eye visible. "What kinda job you got for a bastard?"

"That depends," Johnny said. "Are you the type of bastard who's gonna lay in the field and feel sorry for himself, or are you that same angry young man I was talking with yesterday?"

Peter sat up. "I'm angry."

"Good." Johnny surveyed the land around them. "I got three men out at the cabin Kansas was in. I got three heading to where we think he might be headed. That only leaves me two to stay in there and protect your ma if they decide to come back by the house. I reckon the doc's in there, but ..."

"But what?"

"I never seen him shoot. I've seen what you can do."

Peter looked at him. "What'm I supposed to do?"

"Go find them deputies at the house," Johnny said. "Tell 'em I sent you and to put you where they see fit. Your ma needs folks lookin' out for her right now. It may very well be they tell you to go inside with the doc. They do that, you remember what I told you."

Peter looked at him, eyebrows up.

"There's a lot of ways to care for folks. You do that just natural. Sometimes you'll need a gun, sometimes you'll need a doctor's bag. You're one of the few folks I ever known who I reckon can learn to work with either one of 'em." He paused a moment, letting the words sink in. "So, you the man for that job?"

Peter stood up. "Yes, sir."

"Good," Johnny said. "'Less the doc tells you otherwise, you best let her rest for the time being. When I come back, all three of us will have a talk."

"Yes, sir," Peter turned and raced back toward the house, his feet carrying him just as fast as he'd fled moments before.

Johnny watched him run and, though he'd never been much of a praying man, sent a few words heavenward, hoping he'd made the right decision.

***

It was about an hour's ride to the gold's false location, and when Johnny arrived at the meeting area, he was surprised to see not two, but five men waiting on him.

"Change of plans, I take it?"

"Apparently you're right on time," Wilfred said. "These boys said the gang was already at the cabin when they got there, so they hung back, listening to see what their next move was gonna be."

"Rest of the gang finally arrived, did they?"

Wilfred nodded. "Not much of a gang, but enough. Said they counted another six fellas. So, I figure, now that you decided to show up, we got us a fair fight."

Johnny grinned at the jab. "You think I'd miss this? I worked hard on that map."

"They oughtta be ..." Wilfred stopped, holding up a hand.

In the distance, a few loud voices could be heard, arguing, laughing, hollering.

"Right on time," the deputy said. "I reckon it's up to you now, boss."

Johnny dismounted and looped the reins around a low-hanging tree branch, signaling for the others to follow suit. The group hunkered down between the horses and Johnny outlined their plan as best he could with a few twigs and rocks laying on the ground.

"If we were farther out west, I'd've chosen a box canyon," he said, "but we gotta make do with what we got. The entrance to the mine's right here," he placed a pebble as one of the men beside him let out a quiet laugh. He looked over, eyebrows up.

"Little on the nose ain't it? The gold's in a mine."

Johnny smiled. "Well, where else would you expect to find it? Besides, this far out we ain't gotta worry about nobody but us and them. My bet is we aren't getting out of this without a few bullets flying and, when that's the case, I'd just as soon have the only ones in danger be the trees and the dirt."

The man nodded, still grinning.

"We're gonna line up like so," Johnny placed a few more pebbles out. "You three on the far side, us three over here. Lay low, don't get antsy, and we may make this pretty easy on ourselves.

"Here's the important thing: I know we're all ready for this to be done with, but let 'em get in there for a bit. If you give me the choice between tangling with a fella who's fresh and one who's been digging in the dirt for an hour, I'm gonna take the tired fella every time."

"Not to mention," Wilfred spoke up. "The longer they're in there with nothing, the less they're gonna be keen on taking a bullet for Kansas. Loyalty don't last too long with these fellas if there ain't money involved."

"Exactly," Johnny said. He looked around the group. "Nobody do nothing till you see me make my move. After that," he smiled, "you just do what you're trained to do."

***

Johnny lay on his stomach at the crest of the slope, Wilfred on one side, a deputy from Pineville on the other. It had been almost ninety minutes. The raucous attitude the outlaws had shown when they first filed past and into the mine had slowly but surely been chipped away at just as much as the rock itself.

It was no surprise that Kansas had been the one making the most appearances. The inside of a mine, while it may hold untold wealth, is never a pleasant place to spend one's time. The gang leader had wandered aimlessly in and out, the only change being a rapid reduction in his patience with every new appearance.

From where they were hidden above, the lawmen could hear every word and curse Kansas threw at his men.

"Y'know," Wilfred whispered. "The craziest thing about this whole mess is, them fellas in there actually *want* to be doing this."

"Promise of gold'll get a man to do a lot."

"That's the thing though," the deputy returned. "It's a promise from Dane Kansas. What makes any one of them fellas think they're gonna walk out of here alive?"

Johnny shrugged. "Five to one if he turns on 'em."

"Yeah, well," Wilfred adjusted his position, "old Coy thought he was safe too."

Johnny nodded silently. Whatever may happen to the men down there, the one thing he was most concerned about – the whereabouts of the outlaws – was taken care of. At that moment, Etta and Peter were safe.

The sheriff watched for another quarter hour or so, until voices in the mine rose, not in excitement, but in frustration. Kansas was the first out of the mine, followed quickly by two, three, then all five of the men who had come with him.

"The map says it's there!" Kansas yelled, holding up the paper and jabbing it with his finger. "If you're too lazy to look for it, then go! I don't know what I need any extra men for!"

The man who had apparently incited the incident laughed. "You don't know do ya? I got a pretty good idea. Seems to me you don't know how to work a shovel. I sure ain't see ya pick one up yet."

Wilfred leaned over. "We wait long enough, they may just shoot each other. Save us the job."

Johnny smiled. "You make a good point. But," he reached down and pulled a revolver from its holster. "You wanna cart all them bodies back?"

Before Wilfred could answer, Johnny was up, his gun held out in front of him, his body silhouetted against the setting sun.

"Dane Kansas," the sheriff called out. "You're under arrest on two counts of murder, one count of attempted murder, one count of attempted kidnapping, breaking and entering ..." Johnny chuckled. "Aw shoot, I'm sure we'll come up with some more on the ride back. That oughtta do for now, though."

The outlaws below fell silent, their infighting temporarily forgotten at the surprise of Johnny's appearance.

Only Kansas seemed nonplussed. "Sheriff Steele," he called back. "I wondered if you'd be lurkin' around again. I figured you might be home nursing your whore."

Johnny felt his teeth clench but forced himself to focus on the job. His only duty was to bring this man in, not to react to his jibes.

"It's funny," Kansas continued, slowly folding the map in front of him. "I've been trying to figure out why that woman looked so familiar and it finally came to me earlier today. That boy you've been running with, the one I've been trying to track down myself, what is he, about fifteen?"

"Enough, Kansas," Johnny said, reaching down for his other gun and trying to keep all the men in his field of vision.

"I'm just surprised is all," Kansas said. "That young man running about with a sheriff. And all this time I was told the apple doesn't fall far from the tree. Seems folks must be mistaken after all. I can't say I'm a proud papa though."

That was the tipping point. The man may have sired Peter. He may have taken Etta and left her with a child inside. But he was no *papa*. He had no right to the word. Johnny felt his vision narrow in on the man, could feel the blood pumping in his temples. Almost of its own accord, his right arm brought the barrel of the gun to Kansas's chest, the sights, just as he'd taught Peter, lined up over the man's heart.

"Lotta men to shoot here," Kansas said. "Better hope you're fast. But don't worry," he grinned up at Johnny, "I'll take good care of them both when you're gone."

It was a movement to his left that caught Johnny's eye first. His finger was tensed on the trigger, the pressure moments away from putting an end to Kansas right where he stood. But one of the men, the one closest to the mine, drew first.

Johnny turned left, the gun coming up, sighting, and firing almost simultaneously. He dropped immediately, hitting the dirt at the same time the outlaw stumbled back into the mine entrance, blood spurting from his chest.

Gunfire erupted in the small space. A bullet ripped through the grass where Johnny had just been standing, kicking up dirt a few feet behind him.

Across the ridge, he saw the three deputies spring up, four revolvers and a rifle bursting forth fire from their barrels.

Below, the outlaws, both surprised and confused now, turned aimlessly, firing in all directions at once.

Johnny rolled to his stomach, springing to his feet as Wilfred and the man from Pineville raced past him down the slope. Johnny had eyes for only one man, though. Let the others deal with the rest.

Kansas, taking advantage of the confusion, had rushed immediately away from the mine and headed back toward where they'd hitched their horses on arrival. If he made the saddle, there was no way Johnny could catch up with the man. He'd never rest knowing this monster was out roaming unfettered.

Johnny stretched his legs, heedless of the gunfire, feeling the surge of energy that Peter must have felt just a few hours ago take him.

Kansas was only paces from his horse.

Johnny looked ahead. He'd have one chance. If he timed it right ...

Kansas had a brief moment in the saddle, a split second of time to think he'd made it, before Johnny leaped from the rocky outcropping. He heard as much as he felt the outlaw's collarbone break when his shoulder connected.

The two tumbled to the ground, the horse rearing back and racing off down the path.

Despite his one useless arm, Kansas had managed to pin one of Johnny's underneath himself in the fall. A flash of silver in the dying light and Johnny rolled to the side, six inches of steel stabbing harmlessly into the dirt where he'd just lain.

He grabbed Kansas by the wrist, forcing the man over onto his back, and pinned him to the ground, his knees on the gang leader's shoulders.

Before he realized what he was doing, Johnny felt the soft give of the flesh beneath Kansas's jaw as he pushed his revolver to the man's head.

He felt almost outside himself as he watched his thumb pull back the hammer. It was as if it was another man doing the killing. It would be so simple. Legal even. Kansas was fleeing. A murderer. A rapist. Who would fault him for freeing the world of this man's presence?

Looking up at him, Kansas tried to smile. "It's good ..." he said, the force of the gun making it difficult to speak. "Now, no matter what happens ..." he laughed with a wheeze, "the boy will have a murderer for a father."

Johnny felt his chest rise and fall, slowly. Just like he'd told Peter. Squeeze the trigger when you exhale. Make sure you're focusing on the target. Nothing could be simpler.

He looked down at the man, the pride, the contempt, the evil dancing in Dane Kansas's eyes.

It was a simple move.

Johnny flipped the gun in his hand, bringin the butt across Kansas's temple, cracking the man's head as he'd done to Etta, taking the man's pride as he'd done to Etta. But not taking his life, as Johnny hoped Peter would never do.

Chapter Forty-One

About a week later, Johnny sat at his kitchen table, Peter on one side and Etta, finally feeling stable on her feet, up and about with them. Whether it was in the tumble from the horse or a stray bullet in the firefight beforehand, Johnny had sustained a deep gash in his left arm, which now hung loosely in a sling across his chest. Peter, for his part, couldn't be more proud.

"Got winged, did ya?" he'd asked. "Yeah, that happens sometimes."

Etta laughed. "Oh what would you know about ..." her voice trailed off as she looked between the sheriff and her son, the nearly identical wounds finally becoming clear to her. "Johnathan Steele, is there something you've been keeping from me about my son?"

Just then the front door opened and Wilfred walked in. "Hope I'm not interrupting."

"Couldn't have come at a better time," Johnny laughed. "What brings you over?"

"What else?" the old deputy said. "You can't leave me with a treasure map and not expect me to get antsy."

Johnny gestured to his arm. "You know I'd be there with ya if I could, but I ain't really in riding form."

Wilfred looked at him for a moment. "Now what makes you think I come here looking for you?" He glanced over at Peter. "You got one more adventure in you?"

Peter jumped up, nearly tipping his chair over. Then in an act of self-restraint that couldn't help but bring a smile to Johnny's face, the boy looked at his mother.

Etta sighed. "After what we've been through, as long as you aren't taking him to the Amazon I suppose it's safer than the last few weeks."

Wilfred laughed softly. "No, no, not quite that far. It'll be a bit of a hike, but nothing our young friend ain't been through before."

Peter looked at the deputy, puzzled for a moment. "But you said ..."

Wilfred held up a finger. "I didn't say nothing about nothing. We all sat there and listened. *He* said he didn't know where the gold was. Now maybe he did and maybe he didn't, but the map Johnny found seems to have the last word on it."

"It was up there the whole time?"

Wilfred shrugged. "That's what I aim to find out if you feel like doing a little digging."

Peter looked at Johnny. "And you knew?"

"Hey, now," Johnny held his good hand in front of him. "If I recall, finding a lump of gold wasn't the top of my priority list at the time. Way I figured, until we had Kansas locked up, that gold could just stay hid. It was doing a mighty fine job being outta sight. Besides, like Wilfred said, I was half-inclined to believe Trevor didn't know neither. No sense in draggin' another fella into a mess before we cleaned up the first one." He paused for a moment and then looked at Peter. "But I'll tell ya this, fresh clean water ain't the only thing you might wanna look for around that spring."

Peter's eyes darted around the table, almost as if he couldn't decide where his excitement wanted him to look – his mother for allowing him to go, Johnny for knowing the secret to buried treasure, or Wilfred for being the one who was willing to take him there.

"Go on," Johnny said, laughing. "You look like you're about to pop your top. You're gonna need that energy today. I ain't no psychic, but I see a long walk and a lotta diggin' in your future."

Peter raced toward the door. "C'mon! Wilfred! Let's go!" He was out onto the porch before the old man got up from the table.

"I'll get 'im back to you this evening," he said with a smile.

"Have fun," Johnny laughed. "Try and keep up."

"Let's go!" they heard from outside. "Thanks mom! Bye, Johnny! Bye, mom!"

Etta put her head in her hands and sighed. "What in the world have I gotten myself into with you, John? First he wants to be a lawman, now he wants to be a treasure hunter. What's next? Rodeo clown?"

Johnny laughed and moved around the table to sit beside her. "I got an inkling," he said, "and I tell ya I think it's none of the above. But I'd hate to spoil the surprise."

"Oh, heavens no!" the woman laughed. "Who would you be without your secrets?"

"Listen," Johnny said, taking her hand with his good one. "Something I wanna talk to you about regarding that." He took a breath, steadying himself. "I know you seen some photos laying about here, and I appreciate that you haven't asked me much about myself or who I am. But I've been thinking, maybe it's time you knew ..."

Once the words had begun, he found it much easier than he'd imagined. It wasn't so much giving himself away as it was sharing who he was. He wasn't losing his past and replacing it with something else; he was expanding it, enriching it. Etta's kind eyes taking in every word, he hand holding his throughout. This wasn't a woman in competition with someone who had come before, she was a woman who felt with him, hurt with him, and more than anything, wanted to be beside him through it all, good and bad.

In the end, he looked down at their hands, surprised to see the fingers intertwined. "Maybe that ain't the exact thing you wanted to hear," he said, "but I'd never feel right unless you knew."

"Johnny, I'm honored, but ... why me?"

"Because ..." he sighed. "Well ... you see ..." He laughed a little to himself. "I ain't too good with words. Maybe this'll help."

He looked up at her and, taking her chin in his hand, tilted her head back slightly and leaned in, pressing his lips to hers.

He felt her relax in his arms, could sense the way she leaned into him, with all that she was, as if this was the only place either of them ever needed to be.

"Wait," she said, her lips brushing his.

"What?"

"What about the treasure?"

He laughed, kissing the corner of her mouth. "I found mine right here."

Epilogue

Ten Years Later

"You may think you know folks," Johnny said to Peter as they walked up the path toward the house, "but I've got years of experience on you. And that right there," he pointed to where Etta and another woman sat in rocking chairs, "is trouble ten times over."

Peter laughed. "Ma, Ms. Peters, or both?"

Johnny grinned. "This may be a divide and conquer type situation."

Etta, catching sight of the men, held up a hand. "Welcome home. How was work?"

"Fine," they answered simultaneously, bringing another bit of laughter from the two women.

"You didn't kill nobody today, did ya?" Miss Peters asked, a mischievous grin on her face.

"That ones all yours," Johnny said.

Before Peter could answer, a little dark-haired girl came running out of the house. Her hair was up in pig-tails, a doll clasped to her chest. "Daddy!"

"And that one's all yours," Peter said, stepping back as the girl took a running leap into Johnny's arms.

"I missed you!" the girl yelled, giggling as Johnny worked his fingers up and down her ribs.

"I missed you too, young lady. You been minding your ma?"

"A'course," she said between laughs.

Johnny looked over at Etta, who simply raised an eyebrow. "Well, mostly minding your ma is a start. You at least ain't been causing no trouble have ya?"

Etta laughed. "You expect your daughter to say 'no' to that?"

"All right, all right," Johnny sat the girl down. "I'll come find ya in a minute. Let me say hello to your mother first."

"And Aunt Jenny!"

Johnny grinned as the young Miss Peters blushed.

"Ain't gonna be 'Aunt' Jenny," Peter said, flushing slightly himself. "I reckon she'll be moret of a sister to ya. Do you know how many days?"

"Three!" the girl yelled and then bolted back inside. "I'll be a flower girl!" echoed out the door after her.

Johnny looked at Peter. "I think she's excited."

"That makes three of us," Jenny said, grinning over at Peter.

"Five," Johnny said, looking at Etta, his son, and his soon to be daughter-in-law. It was something he thought he'd given up on long ago, something life had seemed to tease him with before pulling it away every time. Now, here, he finally had a family.

He reached over and patted Peter on the shoulder. "C'mon inside for a second, Doc. Wanna show ya something."

THE END

Also by Zachary McCrae

Thank you for reading **"The Witness"**!

If you liked this book, you can also check out **my full Amazon Book Catalogue at:**
https://go.zacharymccrae.com/bc-authorpage

Thank you!